DRACOPEDIA
FIELD GUIDE

WILHELMVS OCONNORI

ARTIFEX NATVRÆ

DRACOPÆDIA

sive

HISTORIA , LEXICON,
SYSTEMA NATVRÆ, ᴱᵀ

DRACONES DE MVNDO

ILLVSTRATO

F&W, IMPACTVM
IONDON, PARIS, ROMA
MMXVIII

DRACOPEDIA
FIELD GUIDE

WILLIAM O'CONNOR

IMPACT
CINCINNATI, OHIO
IMPACTuniverse.com

CONTENTS

Note from the Editor 7

A Note from the Editor

THE STAFF OF NORTH LIGHT AND IMPACT BOOKS was shocked and deeply saddened to learn of the sudden passing of artist William O'Connor in early 2018, shortly after he began work on the *Dracopedia Field Guide*. Bill was thought of fondly by all who worked with him on his five previous books, and we will miss him dearly.

We would like to thank Jeff Menges for his gracious and invaluable assistance in helping us complete Bill's vision for this book, and for inviting many of Bill's colleagues and friends to participate as contributors. We would also like to thank Jeff's wife, Lynne Menges, for her support and review of the book's text during the writing process.

The following artists have our sincerest thanks for providing artwork for this project: Samantha O'Connor, Tom Kidd, Scott Fischer, Donato Giancola, Dan dos Santos, Mark Poole, David O. Miller, Jeremy McHugh, Pat Lewis, Jeff A. Menges, Christine Myshka and Rich Thomas.

Our best wishes go out to Bill's family and friends. The scope of the world that this fantastic artist invented with *Dracopedia* is incredible, and we will always remember him and his beautiful, imaginative creations.

Noel Rivera
Managing Content Director
North Light & IMPACT Books

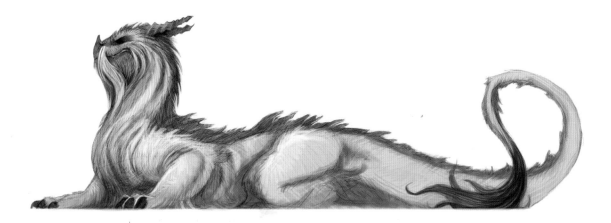

Striped Amphiptere
Pencil and digital
14" × 22" (36cm × 56cm)

AMPHIPTERE

Draco amphipteridae

BIOLOGY

The winged serpent, a common dragon, is a legless serpent with leather wings, ranging from tiny 6" (15cm) garden asps to larger specimens of 6' (183cm). The bat-like wings of the amphiptere allow the creature to travel a range of large distances, but the amphiptere does not usually soar like a bird; rather, it covers its ground using short flying and gliding. The amphiptere's coloration varies greatly from species to species, and it feeds primarily on small creatures such as insects, bats, birds and mice.

Amphiptere in Flight
The amphiptere is rarely mistaken for a bird in flight. Its sinuous tail is both an identifying trait and its chief tool in catching prey.

Amphiptere Habitat
Deep woods and forests are the natural habitat of the amphiptere, but some may also be found living in urban environments.

**Amphiptere Egg,
4" (10cm)**
The amphiptere makes its
nests high in trees, but also
has been known to use the
nests of other birds.

Coming in hundreds of varieties, in various sizes, colors and shapes, and ranging in habitat all over the world, the winged serpent is one of the most common wild members of the dragon class.

The amphiptere is found in all temperate to tropical countries (except Ireland). Today, amphiptere are commonly kept as pets. Rare and beautiful species of winged serpents with exotic patterns are popular in the black markets of Malaysia and India, and imported to Europe and North America. This illegal trade has introduced amphipteridae into ecosystems not intended to support them.

BEHAVIOR

Amphipteridae spend most of their lives in trees and forests. Nesting in high branches, the amphiptere glides between trees, catching insects and small rodents. In this respect the amphiptere is a welcome creature to most farmers. Unfortunately, some amphiptere will find its way into the nests of other birds, looking for eggs. In the henhouses of domesticated chickens, cross-fertilization often occurs, which can result in the hatching of a half-amphiptere, half-chicken, commonly known as a cockatrice. The cockatrice is viewed as a scourge and killed on sight all over the world. Its terrible appearance is responsible for the mythology that its gaze can paralyze its prey to stone, thus erroneously placing it in close relationship to the basilisk (see chapter 8).

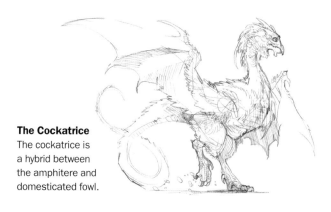

The Cockatrice
The cockatrice is
a hybrid between
the amphitere and
domesticated fowl.

HISTORY

The amphiptere has historically been regarded as a creature of mixed fortune, and today it's a greatly misunderstood animal. Since they live on a diet of vermin, the amphiptere is a welcome addition in cities, and there are many that live in New York City, making nests in the high perches of skyscrapers. The endless supply of rats, mice and pigeons help keep urban areas free of the diseases spread by vermin.

The Grip of a Snake
The amphiptere's slender body can be wrapped around tree limbs,
allowing it to snatch its unsuspecting prey.

SWALLOWTAIL AMPHIPTERE

Easily identified by its unique split tail, the swallowtail amphiptere is commonly found in rural environments, where it can be seen as both an aid and a hindrance. While it will keep rodents in check, it is not above occasionally taking smaller livestock as well.

SPECIFICATIONS
Amphipterus viperacaudiduplexu

Wingspan: 6' (2m)

Distribution: Worldwide, temperate climates

Recognition: Distinctive split tail; bold striping; forward nasal horn

Habitat: Rural areas, large fields

Diet: Insects, smaller mammals and reptiles

Common names: Field Fiend, Darter

Conservation status: Common

FIREWING AMPHIPTERE

The firewing's tail features a dorsal-like winglet that gives it outstanding maneuverability and an advantage in tight, dense spaces that another species might be unable to navigate. It is especially quick and elusive.

SPECIFICATIONS
Amphipterus viperapennignus

Wingspan: 5' (1.5m)

Distribution: Asia, India and Southeast Asia

Recognition: Bright, elongated head crest; spoon-shaped tail

Habitat: Dense jungle

Diet: True scavenger, will eat almost anything

Common name: Blaze

Conservation status: Threatened

MOTHWING AMPHIPTERE

The mothwing is called such because of its tendency to rest its wings in an open, rather than folded, position when still. Its desire to catch more of the sun's heat has evolved into a characteristic trait.

SPECIFICATIONS
Amphipterus viperablattus

Wingspan: 1' (30cm)

Distribution: Northern Asia and Scandinavia

Recognition: Open wings when resting, rarely folded

Habitat: Scrub, light forest

Diet: Insects, small rodents, fish

Common names: Red Whip, Flicker

Conservation status: Uncommon

GARDEN AMPHIPTERE

The most common of the group, the garden amphiptere has wide distribution and can prosper in almost any climate. With subtle variations in patterns and wing shape, it is the variety most likely seen by the farmer or in a suburban setting.

SPECIFICATIONS
Amphipterus viperahortus

Wingspan: 1' (30cm)

Distribution: Near worldwide

Recognition: Jagged tail fin; beak-like jaws

Habitat: Any forested area

Diet: Insects and small rodents most common prey due to smaller size

Common names: Dusty Rose, Jagged Hook Wing

Conservation status: Common

VULCAN AMPHIPTERE

Preferring higher, rocky environments for nesting, this amphiptere was first discovered on the slopes of Mount Aetna in Sicily, which is where its Roman label originated. Though they are often found near volcanic areas, it is the loose rock that draws them, not the volcanic activity.

SPECIFICATIONS
Amphipterus viperavulcanus

Wingspan: 8' (2.5m)

Distribution: West Coast of Africa and Mediterranean

Recognition: Deep red coloring; large arcing wing shape

Habitat: Higher elevations, rocky and wooded environments

Diet: Mammals, reptiles, birds

Common names: Red Moon, Blood Angel

Conservation status: Endangered

STARBURST AMPHIPTERE

A coastal scavenger, the starburst uses its long, narrow snout to dig for shellfish on sandy beaches. Occasionally dieting on fish as well, it can be a nuisance to fishermen. Its small and forward-facing nasal horn is used to break eggs and open shells.

SPECIFICATIONS
Amphipterus viperacometus

Wingspan: 4'.(1.2m)

Distribution: Pacific Rim

Recognition: High contrast red and ivory coloring; long, thin snout

Habitat: Coastal areas, will sometimes attach itself to a boat

Diet: Shellfish, eggs, marine animals

Common names: Firewisp, Crooner, Red Digger

Conservation status: Uncommon

STRIPED AMPHIPTERE

Common in forested environments, the striped amphiptere often competes with avian raptors for the small mammals of the forest. On rare occasions such competition can result in spectacular territorial battles.

SPECIFICATIONS
Amphipterus viperasignus

Wingspan: 3' (1m)

Distribution: Temperate climates, worldwide

Recognition: Wing striping from red to brown, gradual from front to back; tapering tail has two barbs near wing base

Habitat: Forest and field

Diet: Small rodents

Common names: Thorntail, Striper

Conservation status: Common

GOLDEN AMPHIPTERE

The enlarged wings and great size of the golden amphiptere allow it to soar for great distances. Though rare, it has been identified in all areas of the globe, unafraid to cross a vast plain, mountain range or even an ocean.

SPECIFICATIONS
Amphipterus viperaurulentus

Wingspan: 10' (3m)

Distribution: South and Central America

Recognition: Bright golden color

Habitat: Brushland, farmland

Diet: Small herd animals

Common name: Wheatwing

Conservation status: Critically endangered

Temple Dragon
Pencil and digital
14" × 22" (36cm × 56cm)

ASIAN DRAGON
Draco cathaidae

BIOLOGY

The Asian dragon family includes a wide variety of long, serpentine, four-legged dragons with prehensile tails. Asian dragons are unique in that they are in the order of flightless dragons *(Terradracia)* like drakes but are capable of limited flight. The reason for this is because they do not possess dedicated appendages for flight like dragons and dragonettes. Instead, an Asian dragon uses a unique construction of frills along its body to glide or "swim" through the air.

Asian dragons come in a wide variety of colors, sizes and shapes, and can live in a wide range of habitats, from the mountains of the Tibetan Himalayas to the jungles of Vietnam to the Philippines and into India.

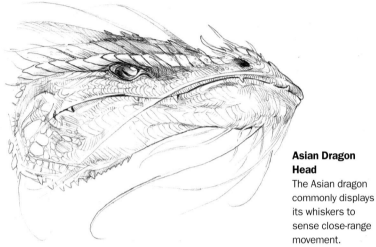

Asian Dragon Head
The Asian dragon commonly displays its whiskers to sense close-range movement.

Because of the Asian dragon's similarity to the Arctic dragon, many species are often miscategorized. This mistake is understandable since the Asian and Arctic dragon species share some habitats in Asia and are often

Asian Dragon Habitat
Bamboo forests provide an ideal environment, but their gradual disappearance is limiting the habitat of Asian dragons.

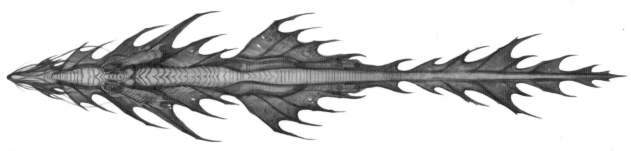

Asian Dragon Overhead
A definitive look at the frilled wings on an Asian temple dragon as seen from above.

depicted interchangeably in classical Asian art. However, the two families are very different. Asian dragons do not grow fur, nor do they live above the Arctic Circle. Arctic dragons in turn do not have the gliding ability of the Asian species or a prehensile tail.

Asian dragons are omnivores, eating fruits, bamboo and meat as it is available. In the winter in the northern areas of its range, the Asian dragon will migrate to warmer climates.

BEHAVIOR

Although there are a great number of species, the Asian dragon is a solitary and remote creature keeping to uninhabited areas of deep forest. Living in the dense forests of Asia with an ample food supply of small animals and fruits to choose from allows the Asian dragon to grow up to 30' (9m) in length. Its main rival as the alpha predator is the tiger and other large cats. The Asian dragon is an agile and powerful fighter. The long serpentine body is able to constrict around an enemy, similar to the wyrm, and its four legs are equipped with sharp talons for fighting. They have a jaw of sharp teeth, and a few species possess the ability to spit a caustic expectorant to frighten enemies. If the Asian dragon were not so reclusive and shy, it would be far more dangerous to humans, but there are very few injuries attributed to it.

Asian Dragon Egg, 8' (20cm)
A rich ivory to an antique gold, and very even in surface finish. The egg of the Asian dragon is revered as a magical object.

HISTORY

Beautiful and elegant creatures, the Asian dragons are revered in many Eastern countries and are heralded as sacred animals in the Shinto, Hindu and Buddhist religions. The depictions of the Asian dragon in art, architecture, clothing and crafts are extensive throughout all Asian countries, and references in libraries and museums are readily available.

The smaller variants of Asian dragon, such as the bonsai and fuji species, have long been kept and bred in Asian cultures as traditional companions to emperors and powerful warlords.

Today, the Asian dragon is protected by the governments of China, Vietnam, Korea and Japan. Although they are difficult to keep alive in captivity, the Hong Kong Zoological and Botanical Gardens has a breeding pair of Asian temple dragons in their collection and hope to have offspring soon. In Europe and America it is illegal to privately own any species or breed of Asian dragon without a permit.

There is, however, a lucrative trade in Asian dragons intended for illegal zoos, private collections and illegal dragon fighting. The tradition of using Asian dragons for fighting goes back centuries, but the governments of Thailand, Myanmar and China, along with a consortium of other dragon conservation trusts led by the World Dragon Protection Fund, have collaborated to put a stop to illegal Asian dragon trafficking and fighting. It is believed that thousands of Asian dragons have been saved as the result of such efforts.

JADE DRAGON

TEMPLE DRAGON

SPECIFICATIONS
Cathaidaus rangoonii

Size: 3' (91cm)

Distribution: Southeast Asia

Recognition: Long, frilled green body with green markings

Habitat: Mountainous jungles and rainforests

Diet: Omnivore

Common names: Rangoon Serpent, Miner's Dragon

Conservation status: Critically endangered

The jade dragon was once found throughout most of Southeast Asia in the nations of Cambodia, Thailand and Myanmar, where the diminutive species was kept as a good luck pet for the Kachinland jade miners for thousands of years. Extensive jade mining devastated the jade dragon's ecosystem, but protective dragon sanctuaries in Asia have been developed to protect this endangered dragon species.

SPECIFICATIONS
Cathaidaus dracotemplum

Size: 30' (9m)

Distribution: Southern Asia, including India and Southeast Asia

Recognition: Its unusual locomotion is its most distinct feature

Habitat: Mountain forests, temples, shrines and monasteries

Diet: Omnivore

Common names: Ribbon Dragon, Temple Dragon

Conservation status: Critically endangered

For as long as can be remembered, the temple dragon has been a presence in the realm of man. Its influence and representation in art go back thousands of years. It is believed by some that an extended family of these extraordinary creatures thrived centuries ago in a monastery in the Eastern Shandong Province of China, bringing us the species we know today.

BONSAI DRAGON

Bred extensively as a pet throughout Asia for its diminutive size, the tiny bonsai dragon is now effectively extinct in the wild, but still popular as a status pet by the new emerging upper classes in Asia. Bred in a range of colors and patterns, in its natural form the bonsai dragon takes on a mottled pattern of earth tones.

SPECIFICATIONS
Cathaidaus penjingus

Size: 14" (36cm)

Distribution: Asia

Recognition: Small size, irregular frilling

Habitat: Forest, bamboo groves

Diet: Omnivore

Common names: Ratling, Penji

Conservation status: Extinct in the wild

IMPERIAL DRAGON

The imperial dragon was revered as a sacred animal since the first emperors of China's Tang Dynasty. Today's imperials are the descendants of those royal dragon houses. Though there have been reported wild sightings in the Cangshan mountains of Yunnan recently, these have been largely unverified.

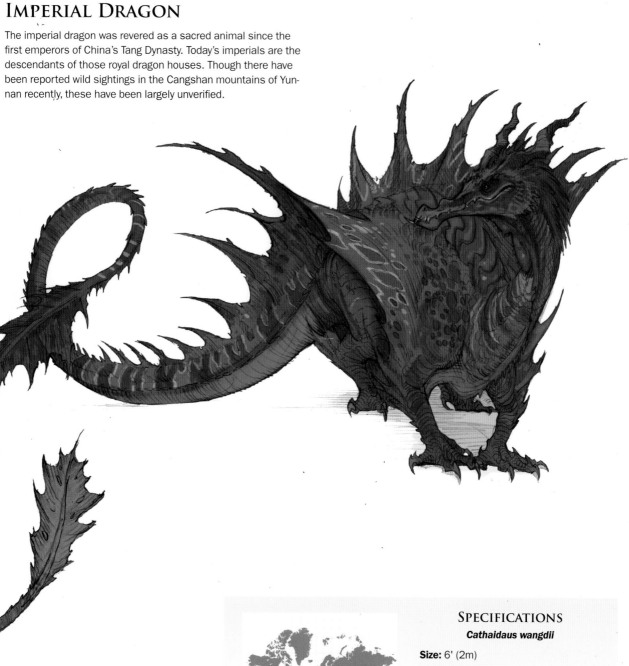

SPECIFICATIONS

Cathaidaus wangdii

Size: 6' (2m)

Distribution: China

Recognition: Deep red overall color; tall, double spine frill

Habitat: Forest

Diet: Omnivore

Common name: Blood Guard

Conservation status: Extinct in the wild

KOREAN DRAGON

A great climber and true forest dragon, the Korean dragon seeks a vantage point from high in cliff faces or treetops, and is wary of approaching threats. Once a species that caused travelers to fear that wooded areas were haunted, the Korean dragon is now endangered and rarely encountered.

SPECIFICATIONS
Cathaidaus goguryeoyongii

Size: 4' (1.2m)

Distribution: Southeast Asia, especially Korean peninsula

Recognition: Earthy-gray; leafy frills with a distinct blue-green hue to the cranial crest

Habitat: Forest, higher elevations and mountainous regions

Diet: Omnivore, smaller mammals such as shrews, moles, hares and bats

Common names: Yong, Goguryeo Dragon

Conservation status: Critically endangered

Himalayan Dragon

The Himalayan dragon is one of the few Asian dragons that still thrives in the wild due, in part, to its habitat being so remote and inhospitable.

A protective sanctuary was established in 1999 inside the Shey Phoksundo National Park in Nepal. The Himalayan has a healthy presence in the park and is still encountered in the upper reaches of mountains to the west. During long winters it will hide itself away in a near hibernation state to emerge in great numbers during the first warm spring days.

SPECIFICATIONS
Cathaidaus shephoksundus

Size: 5' (1.5m)

Distribution: North Western China, Nepal

Recognition: Dual frills on head and along abdomen

Habitat: Subalpine forest

Diet: Omnivore

Common names: Sleeping Dragon, Dream Thief, Blue Shepko

Conservation status: Endangered

SPIRIT DRAGON

The white, spirit or ghost dragon was considered a myth until its discovery in the late 19th century by European explorers to the Asian interior. Avoiding contact with man, the white dragon eluded study until recently when found in the snowy mountains along the Chinese and Nepal border. Unlike its cousin the Himalayan dragon, this creature has remained hidden by the snow and cloud cover in its regional habitat, offering human eyes little more than glimpses over many centuries.

FUJI DRAGON

The rare and elusive Fuji dragon is extremely scarce in the wild, placing it on the near-extinct list. The Fuji dragon is unique in that the only living specimens have been found on the slopes of Mt. Fuji in Japan. This is unusual for Asian dragons, which usually prefer densely populated forests, but the rocky and rugged terrain of the lower volcanic mountain allow this diminutive dragon to hunt small mammals, insects and reptiles. Pilgrims climbing Mt. Fuji take great pride in the rare spotting a Fuji dragon, and it is considered a blessing of good fortune.

SPECIFICATIONS
Cathaidaus yamadoragonus

Size: 16" (41cm)

Distribution: Central Japan, Mt. Fuji

Recognition: Elongated serpentine body with black and blue markings; antlers on males

Habitat: Mountainous

Diet: Omnivore

Common names: Shogun Dragon, Shanlong, Mountain Dragon, Fujidoragon

Conservation status: Near extinct

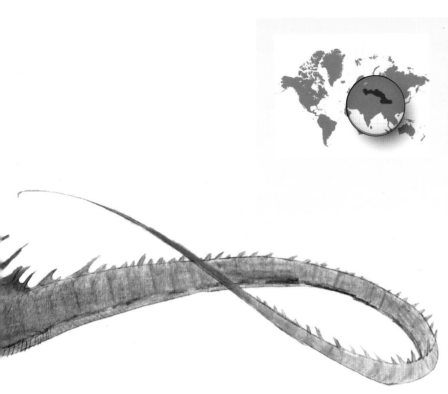

SPECIFICATIONS

Cathaidaus jingshenlongus

Size: 10' (3m)

Distribution: Tibetan Mountains, Nyenchen and Gangtise ranges

Recognition: Large, prominent frill spikes; from white to shadowy blue-gray

Habitat: Snow-covered mountainous regions

Diet: Unknown

Common names: Jingshenlong, Ghost Dragon

Conservation status: Critically endangered

Jormundgander
Pencil and digital
14" × 22" (36cm × 56cm)

SEA ORCS

Draco cetusidae and *Draco dracanquillidae*

BIOLOGY

Evolving from land species of dragons millions of years ago, the sea orc exists in two family groups. The *Dracanguillidae* (dragon eel) are the snake-like species of sea orcs, which have been reputed to grow to titanic lengths in excess of 300' (91m), while the *Cetusidae* is the smaller, more terrestrial family of sea orcs growing to 50' (15m).

Since 75 percent of the surface of the earth is water, sea orcs are the most varied and numerous of the *Draconia* class of animals. There are dozens of species that have been documented; others are nearly extinct and still today there are rare species that have never been seen. Primarily feeding on fish, seals, shellfish and other sea creatures, all sea orcs must return to the surface to breathe. Once a year, the female sea orc crawls to the shore or into the shallows to lay her eggs. This vulnerable time is responsible for the majority of fatalities of both adults and young. Sea orclings are tiny when born but quickly grow to adulthood.

Similar to marine mammals, sea orcs have evolved limbs specialized for swimming, and these marine dragons can grow to massive sizes. The size of its skull demonstrates how this powerful animal can feed easily on even the largest whales and squids in the ocean. The long, interlocking teeth allow it to snatch at fish. Able to dive to tremendous depths, sea orcs are the natural enemies of the giant squid, sperm whales and large sharks.

Sea Orc Egg
Despite the colorful and varied appearances of the sea orcs, their eggs are simple and often difficult to identify.

Sea Orc Habitat
A peaceful, sandy beach may easily hide a large number of sea orcs just out of sight.

BEHAVIOR

The habitat of the Atlantic sea orc ranges in the northern waters stretching from Cape Cod, Massachusetts, to the Irish Sea and fjords of Norway. In the winter the sea orc migrates south to take up its hunting grounds in the Bahamas. The saltwater sea orc has been reported to attack ships plying the northern sealanes since the 15th century. Some accounts of sea orc attacks in the southern Atlantic have been accredited to the mysterious disappearance of ships in the Bermuda Triangle. Today the Atlantic Faeroe sea orc is a rare find, having been hunted to near extinction throughout the 19th and 20th centuries; it is now protected as an endangered species.

HISTORY

The word *orc* comes from the Latin *Orcus*, which means both *whale* and *the underworld*. This is also where the killer whale gets the name orca. The most famous sea orc

Jormundgander Head
Possibly the largest serpent species in the sea, Jormundgander is the source of many legendary tales.

is, of course, the Loch Ness monster, which is a Scottish sea orc. A similar account of the Scottish sea orc is in *Orlando Furioso* by Ariostos, in which the maidens Angelica and Olympia are to be sacrificed to a sea orc near the Isle of Skye in Scotland. The hero Orlando stops the creature when he wedges a ship's anchor into the creature's mouth. Although some marine biologists suggest that the famous kraken of ancient mythology was a sea orc, it is believed that the kraken was in fact a giant squid. The titanic leviathan is also often mistaken for a sea orc, but it is believed to actually be a cetacean.

The largest specimen of a saltwater sea orc is in Greenwich, England, at the National Maritime Museum. This 225' (69m) specimen was killed in the Irish Sea by the frigate HMS *Pertinacious* in 1787.

Jormundgander

This enigmatic sea dragon has been the subject of legend for centuries. It was believed to be extinct or merely myth until a carcass of a 200' (61m) specimen washed up on the coast of Spain in 1927. Related to the Faeroe sea orc, it is believed to spend most of its life at extreme depths of the oceans hunting squid and other deep sea creatures. Because of its rarity, and lack of contemporary evidence, the Jormundgander sea orc has never been documented in the wild. Draconologists believe that it is the only sea orc species to lay its eggs in the ocean, allowing its young to be born in the water and leading to its scarcity due to the predation of eggs and hatchlings.

Scottish Sea Dragon

Specifications
Cetusidus orcidius

Size: 40'–70' (12m–21m)

Distribution: Northern Hemisphere, northern seas and major lakes of Scotland, Iceland and Scandinavia

Recognition: Long sinuous neck; large flippers for swimming; spinal frill

Habitat: Deep, cold water lakes

Diet: Small fish, vegetation

Common names: Nessie, Champ, Ogopogo, Lagarfljótsormur

Conservation status: Uncommon

SPECIFICATIONS

Dracanquillidus jormundgandus

Size: 500' (152m)

Distribution: Colder to moderate waters, worldwide

Recognition: Blue-green color; frilled head

Habitat: Deep sea

Diet: Squid, whale

Common names: Thorsbane, Jormun

Conservation status: Extinct

A brackish-water sea dragon, the Scottish sea dragon may be found inland among freshwater lakes. It is known to travel from one body of water to another nearby, although it is quite vulnerable on land and will only come ashore under the cover of night. Because of this behavior, some draconologists consider it more closely related to the sea lion (see chapter 3) than the sea orc. Reclusive in nature, the Scottish sea dragon avoids contact with larger animals and relies largely on a diet of grasses and small fish. Once thought to have been extinct, new evidence points to a small number that are still present in colder bodies of water.

Sea Lion

There is no confusing this dragon species with the mammal that shares its name. The draconian sea lion can be found in shallow waters and coastal areas worldwide, and, unlike the sea orc that spends its entire life in the water, it gravitates to rugged coastline where it seeks shelter, hunts and lays eggs among the rocks and caves. However, it is a powerful hunter, and the draconian sea lion's jaw has been known to break through wooden ship hulls and snap oars, and can pose a threat to almost anything in the water.

SPECIFICATIONS
Cetusidus leodracus

Size: 15' (5m)

Distribution: Worldwide

Recognition: Powerful forelimbs; distinctive dorsal spikes; striping

Habitat: Rocky coastline

Diet: Carnivore

Common names: Sea Hag, Ketea

Conservation status: Least concern

Hammerhead Sea Orc

This large aggressive sea orc lives throughout most of the world's oceans. It has been the scourge of fishermen for centuries, devouring huge numbers of cod and other food fish from North America to Europe. Hunted throughout the 19th century, the hammerhead became a rare sight until its placement on the endangered list in the 1970s.

Draconologists have speculated about the function of the unique hammerhead crest that gives this sea orc its name. Some believe that it's used during mating or for self-protection during hunting, but recent studies have discovered that the hammerhead crest holds a significant amount of sensory organs, allowing it to hunt and detect prey from up to 5 miles (8km) away.

SPECIFICATIONS
Dracanquillidus malleuscaputus

Size: 25' (8m)

Distribution: North Atlantic

Recognition: Broad hammerhead crest; long eel-like tail

Habitat: Oceans

Diet: Carnivore

Common names: Pick Axe, Boomer, Anchorhead

Conservation status: Endangered

FRILLED SEA ORC

This aggressive and beautiful deep-water sea dragon has been the longing of deep-sea fishermen for hundreds of years. Today, sport fishing for prized sea orcs is a big business, with prices for the meat exceeding their weight in gold in Japan. The 1995 World Fisheries Act, along with the World Dragon Protection Fund, attempted to protect these animals from overfishing, but poachers in unregulated waters routinely illegally hunt these sea dragons. Today, sea dragons like the frilled and striped have become immensely popular in pop culture as TV shows like *Dragonhooked*, a cable fishing show, have spiked the popularity of sport sea dragon fishing around the world.

SPECIFICATIONS

Dracanquillidus segementumii

Size: 30' (9m)

Distribution: North Atlantic

Recognition: Long snout; frilled fins

Habitat: Deep ocean

Diet: Carnivore, sardines and mackerel

Common name: Blue Seadragon

Conservation status: Endangered

FAEROE SEA ORC

The largest verified serpent, the Faeroe sea orc was once more common throughout Atlantic waters, but today, it appears in the Northern waters between Norway and Greenland. The concentration of sightings in this area is what has given this beast its name.

Until the early 1900s, the Faeroe sea orc had been hunted in an annual rite by some Scandinavian fishing communities. Today, this species remains under protection. Sightings have been recorded in the waters north of Iceland more than in recent decades.

SPECIFICATIONS

Dracanquillidus faeroeus

Size: 200' (61m)

Distribution: Atlantic Ocean

Recognition: Long serpentine body

Habitat: Deep ocean water

Diet: Carnivore

Common names: Egede's Serpent, Devil's Tail

Conservation status: Endangered

ELECTRIC SEA ORC

One of the only species of sea orc that lives in fresh water, the electric sea orc, much like its eel cousin, shocks its prey with electricity to disable it. Because of the size of the electric sea orc, animals as large as buffalo have been killed by the shocks of these deadly water dragons, and humans who live near its habitat routinely fall prey to deadly attacks.

SPECIFICATIONS
Dracanquillidus electricus

Size: 12' (4m)

Distribution: Amazon and sub-Saharan African rivers

Recognition: Spear-like bill and multi-color body

Habitat: Shallow fresh water rivers and lakes

Diet: Carnivore

Common names: Lightning Fish, Tesla's Coil

Conservation status: Threatened

FLYING SEA ORC

The flying sea orc is one of the most common and smallest of the *orcadracidae* family of dragons. These sea orcs school in the thousands. Misclassified as a fish for centuries, the flying sea orc is a natural evolution of terrestrial dragons that took to the sea looking for ample food. Caught by the hundreds in tropical and subtropical waters of the Atlantic and Pacific oceans, the flying sea orc is one of few dragons with "least concern" conservation status. Coming ashore every year by the thousands to lay their eggs, they are common prey to predators and humans alike and are often used for sushi and other delicacies.

SPECIFICATIONS
Dracanquillidus fluctusalotorus

Size: 16" (41cm)

Distribution: South Pacific and Atlantic

Recognition: Fin-like wings

Habitat: Tropical and subtropical waters

Diet: Carnivore

Common names: Wave Dragon, Flying Dragonfish

Conservation status: Least concern

Striped Sea Orc

Considered by many draconologists to be one of the most dangerous of all the dragon species, this fast and highly predatory sea orc hunts for fish, seals and other sea dragons in the warm southern Pacific waters near Australia. The large radius of a striped sea orc bite allows the dragon to hunt large prey with sudden, swift attacks, taking mortal bites from larger animals even as large as whales.

SPECIFICATIONS
Dracanquillidus marivenatorus

Size: 25' (8m)

Distribution: South Pacific

Recognition: Distinctive green and pink striping

Habitat: Warm waters

Diet: Carnivore

Common names: Sea Tiger, King Krait

Conservation status: Threatened

Manta Sea Orc

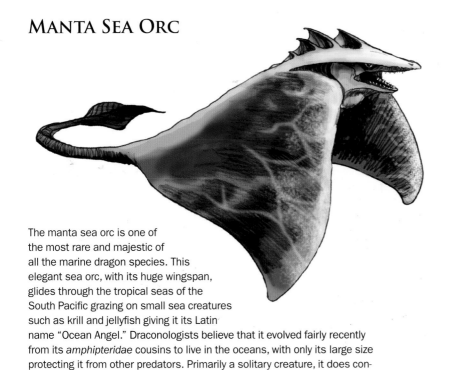

The manta sea orc is one of the most rare and majestic of all the marine dragon species. This elegant sea orc, with its huge wingspan, glides through the tropical seas of the South Pacific grazing on small sea creatures such as krill and jellyfish giving it its Latin name "Ocean Angel." Draconologists believe that it evolved fairly recently from its *amphipteridae* cousins to live in the oceans, with only its large size protecting it from other predators. Primarily a solitary creature, it does congregate in flocks for breeding. It comes ashore on islands to lay it eggs.

SPECIFICATIONS
Dracanquillidus oceanusangelus

Size: 12' (4m)

Distribution: South Pacific

Recognition: Wide, wing-like fins; white-veined skin

Habitat: Tropical oceans

Diet: Carnivore

Common names: Hooded Orc, Night Cloak, Ocean Angel

Conservation status: Critically endangered

Monarch Feydragon
Pencil and digital
14" × 22" (36cm × 56cm)

FEYDRAGON

Draco dracimexidae

BIOLOGY

Anyone with a flower garden is familiar with the fey-dragon. Despite misconceptions and its Latin name, the feydragon is not an insect, but actually belongs in the

Draconia class. The forearms have evolved into a second set of wings, and the legs and feet have developed long digits for grappling prey and holding onto small limbs.

The feydragon flies like an insect or hummingbird rather than a dragon. Its wings flap so quickly that it is able to hover in midair like a helicopter. Its four wings give it the ability to move in any direction while holding position.

Feydragon Egg, ½" (1cm)
The egg is no bigger than the size of a pea. The feydragon can lay many eggs at a time, although most will be eaten by predators and insects.

Feydragon Grip
The feet of the feydragon are long and slender in order to perch on slim branches.

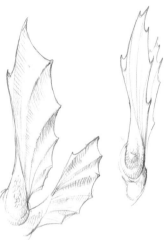

Variation in Flight
The four wings of the fey-dragon act like the rotors of a helicopter, allowing the creature to hover and move in all directions. When at rest the wings fold against the body like fans.

Feydragon Habitat
Feydragons thrive in rural areas, often benefiting from the livestock feed and the farmed fruits and vegetables.

A variety of species of feydragons exist throughout the world in a kaleidoscope of colors and shapes. This carnivorous creature will eat insects, but also go after larger prey such as dragonflies and hummingbirds.

Behavior

Although the tiniest of the dragons, the feydragon has many of the same habits as its larger cousins. Hunting insects in the evening and early morning hours, feydragons will build nests in rocky overhangs or trees, but they prefer to live in the cool, dark woods. Northern breeds of feydragon will not migrate in the winter, but rather hibernate. The feydragon will mate in flight using its brightly colored wings or phosphorescent tail to lure a partner. Like their much larger cousins, the great dragons, feydragons will steal small shiny objects to line their nests.

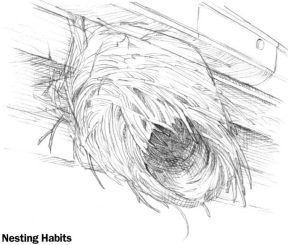

Nesting Habits
Feydragons are capable of building complex and intricately designed homes in which to lay their eggs, often finding suitable locations inside barns or under the eaves of roofs.

History

The feydragon is commonly regarded as the inspiration for almost all fairy and elf tales around the world. Will-o-the-Wisp, brownies, pixies and the like, are all attributed to the playful, colorful and mischievous feydragon. Almost every culture considers it good luck to have a feydragon move into your garden, and many people leave out small offerings of shiny buttons or coins for the diminutive creatures to take.

Human Interaction
Building feyhouses is a popular hobby among dragon enthusiasts.

One of the most famous depictions of a feydragon is from Lewis Carroll's poem "The Jabberwocky" and the illustration by acclaimed Victorian artist John Tenniel. It is obvious by both the name of the poem and the image that the beast is a fantastical incarnation of a leafwing feydragon, sometimes called a Jabberwock for its jabbering chitter. It is also conceivable how the rare deep-woods feydragon could be regarded as a terrifying creature, especially in the eyes of a child.

Today, the feydragon is protected in most regions from capture or harm, and building feydragon gardens is a popular hobby worldwide. Many rural communities, however, have challenged the animal's protection, claiming that the status of the feydragon limits the use of insecticides, leading to the destruction of millions of dollars' worth of agriculture by other pests.

Wraps Like a Rope
The prehensile tail of the feydragon is capable of wrapping around objects to give it better balance.

Leafwing Feydragon

The leafwing feydragon was the inspiration for Lewis Carroll's poem as well as John Tenniel's famous illustration of the Jabberwock. There are varieties of leafwings in distribution the world over. Their demeanor, size and natural camouflage can cause large numbers of them to go practically unnoticed. Until recently, it was a misconception that the leafwing was a solitary feeder. It is now known that they form a community in areas where their numbers are plentiful.

SPECIFICATIONS
Dracimexus pennafoliumus

Size: 10" (25cm)

Wingspan: 8" (20cm)

Distribution: Northwestern Europe

Recognition: Long and spindly; short array of four wings

Habitat: Rural and wooded

Diet: Insects, fruit

Common names: Jabberwock, Leaf Duster, Tree Wisp

Conservation status: Common

Cardinal Feydragon

The cardinal was one of the most sought-after feydragons as a pet in the New World. Their strong red coloring and delicate structure made them quite desirable, and many were captured and brought back to Europe during the 17th and 18th centuries. A small colony took root in northern France as a result, but may now be extinct. The remaining cardinal feydragons prosper in the wilds of Eastern Canada.

SPECIFICATIONS
Dracimexus cardinalis

Size: 10"–12" (25cm–30cm)

Wingspan: 12"–14" (30cm–36cm)

Distribution: Northeast woodlands, North America

Recognition: Bright red markings and head crest on the male; thistle-like, leafy wings

Habitat: Wooded areas, higher altitude

Diet: Fish, small snakes, insects

Common names: Red Wisp, Red Coat

Conservation status: Threatened

Queen Mab Feydragon

Once a prize of the British Isles, the Queen Mab is now a rarity. The Court of Queen Mab, a feydragon preservation group started in Edinburgh in 1932, is dedicated to restoring this and other fey species to their once generous numbers.

SPECIFICATIONS
Dracimexus mercutious

Size: 16"–20" (41cm–51cm)

Wingspan: 12"–14" (30cm–36cm)

Distribution: Scottish Highlands

Recognition: Iridescent blue coloring

Habitat: Woodlands

Diet: Insects, birds, small mammals

Common names: Midnight's Shadow, Blue Devil

Conservation status: Extremely rare

Excalibur Feydragon

This powerful member of the feydragon group is similar in its four-wing structure but differs greatly in other physical aspects. These fey are ground dwellers and will often form packs to attack larger prey. Their powerful legs and wings combine to give them a sort of hyperjump ability, gliding in their descent toward unsuspecting prey.

SPECIFICATIONS
Dracimexus pendragonus

Size: 14" (36cm)

Wingspan: 14"–16" (36cm–41cm)

Distribution: Northern Europe and Asia

Recognition: Dynamic leg structure; rear abdominal pincers

Habitat: Moors, tundra

Diet: Insects, small mammals, birds; groups will sometimes take a much larger animal

Common names: Hop-frog, Ironwing

Conservation status: Low risk

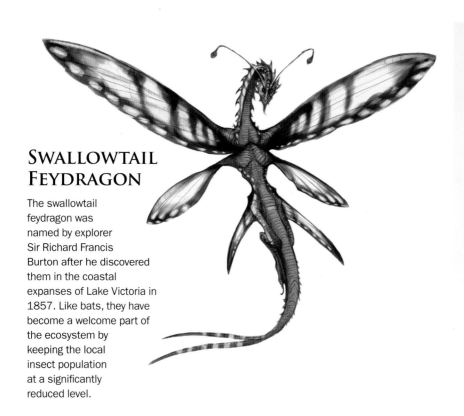

SWALLOWTAIL FEYDRAGON

The swallowtail feydragon was named by explorer Sir Richard Francis Burton after he discovered them in the coastal expanses of Lake Victoria in 1857. Like bats, they have become a welcome part of the ecosystem by keeping the local insect population at a significantly reduced level.

SPECIFICATIONS
Dracimexus furcaudus

Size: 8" (20cm)

Wingspan: 10"–12" (25cm–30cm)

Distribution: Interior and Eastern Africa

Recognition: Long, clean, twin tails; smooth-edged wings

Habitat: Coastal marsh, lakeshores

Diet: Primarily insects

Common names: Forked Skimmer, Burton's Twinspear

Conservation status: Low risk

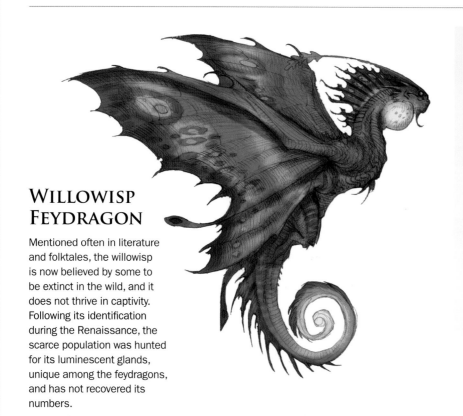

WILLOWISP FEYDRAGON

Mentioned often in literature and folktales, the willowisp is now believed by some to be extinct in the wild, and it does not thrive in captivity. Following its identification during the Renaissance, the scarce population was hunted for its luminescent glands, unique among the feydragons, and has not recovered its numbers.

SPECIFICATIONS
Dracimexus Luminus

Size: 9" (23cm)

Wingspan: 10" (25cm)

Distribution: Previously through-out Eurasia; now greatly reduced

Recognition: Butterfly-like wings; dewlap and tail which can produce a glow

Habitat: Marsh

Diet: Insects, berries, seeds

Common names: Will o' the Wisp, Pan's Dragon

Conservation status: Critically endangered; possibly extinct

SPECIFICATIONS
Dracimexus monarchus

Size: 10" (25cm)

Wingspan: 10"–12" (25cm–30cm)

Distribution: Temperate zones, worldwide

Recognition: Burnt orange highlights, club tail used to strike prey

Habitat: Rural, wooded areas

Diet: Small mammals, eggs, birds

Common name: Crop-duster

Conservation status: Threatened

MONARCH FEYDRAGON

Originally native to North America, the monarch has found its way into most temperate zones, transported by the spread of human exploration. It was once a favorite in royal courts and zoos worldwide, admired for its size and coloring, but, like the willowisp, it rarely survives in captivity. Today it is protected in the United States and Canada.

Welsh Dragon
Pencil and digital
14" × 22" (36cm × 56cm)

GREAT DRAGONS

Draco dracorexidae

BIOLOGY

The eight great dragons are, by far, the most feared and famous creatures in the history of the world. From the beginning of time, the great dragon species have not only inspired our imaginations but have helped form the very cultures with which they coexist. With 100' (30m) wing-spans and the ability to "breathe" fire, they are the largest and most powerful terrestrial animals that have ever lived.

The dragons come in a wide variety of species and live all over the world, from the rocky shores of the Pacific Northwest to the Mediterranean Sea. Although they are revered by every culture and in every region, today there are few surviving specimens. The bright colors of each species are more pronounced in the males than the females.

Of the many species of the great dragon, the most famous is the Welsh red dragon. Consisting of a large quadrupedal body, a long tail, a serpentine neck, scaled armor, and massive bat-like leather wings, the Welsh red

Great Fire-Breathing Dragons

Of all the dragon species only the *Dracorexus* family is able to "breathe" fire. The great dragon's ability to breathe fire is actually a misnomer. More accurately, the dragon spits fire. Great dragons are able to secrete a highly volatile liquid in a gland behind the mandible. The great dragon is able to spit this liquid up to 100' (30m). Once in contact with oxygen, the liquid quickly oxidizes and bursts into flame. This attack is only possible about once a day, and usually as a last resort defense, allowing the dragon to escape a dangerous situation.

Great Dragon Habitats

Supplying abundant quantities of food, constant strong winds and seclusion, the seaside cliffs of the world are the natural habitats of the great dragon.

dragon is highly intelligent and able to breathe fire; this dragon is the most enigmatic and fascinating creature alive. Although great dragons are unable to speak, they have a long and revered relationship with the people of their territories.

BEHAVIOR

Great dragons are highly territorial and antisocial, even to other dragons. They prefer high cliffs and rocky out-croppings, making their homes along tall palisades over-looking the sea. These lofty and remote vantage points allow for clear observation of their territory, safety from enemies and the ability to take flight. The seaside also allows the dragon to feed from the ocean, snatching tuna, porpoises and even small whales from the water, and bringing them back to its lair. Despite their mas-sive size, dragons do not travel very far from their lairs and only move if the food near their lairs disappears, or if they are threatened by human encroachment.

Human-dragon interaction is actually quite rare, since they do not usually share the same territory. The only natural enemies to the great dragon are humans and wyverns. Once reaching adulthood, a great dragon will leave its mother's lair and find its own nest. Here the male dragon will

begin to prepare for a female. Collecting shiny objects to line the nest, the male great dragon will attract a female using calls and fire displays. Once the eggs are laid, the male dragon will leave the lair to find new territory, leav-ing his land and home to his offspring. Great dragons can lay up to as many as four eggs at a time and can live in excess of five hundred years. They are also capable of hibernating for long periods of time. Waking a sleeping dragon is not recommended.

HISTORY

In recent history, the relationship between humans and great dragons has been almost symbiotic, with much care being given to the needs of dragons. Human sacri-fices were once regarded as necessary, but that practice has all but been abandoned in the western world, and actual accounts of human deaths by dragon attack are extremely rare. The oldest and most ancient great dragon on record is the venerable Tong Long Huo, the ancient gold dragon of China, who is reputed to be over five hundred years old.

Acadian Green Dragon

Biology

The Acadian green dragon is the largest dragon species in North America, growing up to 75' (23m) in length with a wingspan over 85' (26m). The eggs are hatched by the female only once every five years in small clutches of one to three eggs. The female and male live together in a lair on the seashore where the male hunts for food in the ocean while the female guards the lair and her young from predators.

Acadian Green Dragon in Profile, 75' (23m)
These majestic dragons are some of the largest and longest-lived in the world.

The high sea cliffs that are the common home to all the great dragon species of the world provide many advantages. The high windswept perch enables the dragons to take flight easily, with the dragonlings only learning to fly in their third year. The remote cave rookeries or lairs allow protection for the nearly defenseless dragonlings until they learn to fly. The male dragonling then leaves the cave and begins looking for a new lair where he begins a family of his own.

SPECIFICATIONS
Dracorexus acadius

Size: 50'–75' (15m–23m)

Wingspan: 85' (26m)

Weight: 17,000 lbs. (7,700kg)

Distribution: Northeastern North America

Recognition: Bright green markings; feathered frill plumage; nasal and chin horns on males; pale green and yellow markings and no horns on females

Habitat: Coastal areas

Diet: Whales, cetaceans

Common names: Green Dragon, American Dragon, Skogeso Dragon, Groendraak

Conservation status: Endangered

Acadian Green Dragon Plumage
The Acadian green dragon is one of the few great dragon species that has feathers. The male produces bright display plumage to attract females. The nasal horn grows bright red during mating season. The female dragon has dull, mottled colors to camouflage herself.

Acadian Green Dragon Egg, 18" (46cm)
Acadian females can lay up to three eggs at a time once every five years.

Acadian Green Dragon Female Ventral View, Wingspan 85' (26m)
Acadian dragons have the largest wingspan in North America. Females are less colorful than their male counterparts.

Green dragons are extremely long lived, with the oldest specimen, Mowhak, having been first reported in 1768. The hibernation habits of the Acadian green dragon contribute to its longevity. It is believed that a dragon may sleep more than two-thirds of its life, slowing its metabolism for months. Older dragons can enter a kind of torpor and can last years without eating. A mature Acadian green dragon male can weigh up to 17,000 pounds (7,700kg) and needs to eat over 150 pounds (70kg) of meat per day.

BEHAVIOR

The Acadian green dragon, like its other great dragon cousins, makes its habitat along rocky shorelines. The primary diet of the Acadian is the prolific whales and cetaceans of the North Atlantic Ocean, especially killer and pilot whales that migrate to the southern waters in the fall. The Acadian male builds a nest in a rocky cave or outcropping overlooking the sea and begins a complicated mating ritual in the late summer.

HISTORY

The first recorded account of a green dragon was in 1602. Early English colonists found the dragons to be abundant, and there are accounts by early whalers

that green dragons would often swoop down and take captured whales right off their harpoons.

Despite these encounters, the green dragon became a source of pride for early Americans and was often used as a standard during the revolution for strength and independence. Bunker Hill overlooking Boston had at one time been the site of a dragon lair. Benjamin

Overlooking Shores
A large male surveying his territory. Males fluff their feathered frills and make elaborate throaty songs that echo across the inlets and bays.

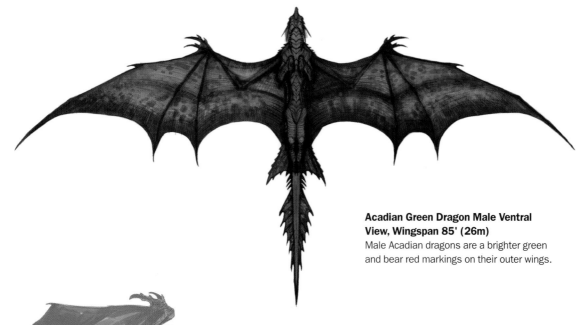

**Acadian Green Dragon Male Ventral
View, Wingspan 85' (26m)**
Male Acadian dragons are a brighter green
and bear red markings on their outer wings.

Flying Displays
During the mating season Acadian green dragons often fly in
pairs showing off for one another. This young bull circled an
uninterested femal for an hour before she finally sent him away
with a puff of fire breath.

Franklin proposed that the green dragon become the
national emblem, but it lost out to the bald eagle.

In the 19th century the whaling and fishing industries
decimated the food fish and whale stocks causing the
dragon population to drop dramatically. The industrialization of many seashore cities like Boston, Portsmouth
and New Haven also destroyed much of the nesting
grounds of the green dragon. By World War II, there
were fewer than 100 green dragons still living, and many
biologists feared that the species had gone extinct.

In 1972, the World Dragon Protection Fund and the
Green Dragon Trust were founded to help raise aware-
ness of the dire situation of the green dragon. In 1993

the Federal Park Service opened Acadia National
Dragon Preserve in Maine, a protected dragon
marine sanctuary adjacent to Acadia National Park.
Since then, other shorelines have become dragon preserves, but inside the Acadia Preserve the green dragon
has been able to flourish. Today, with similar controls on
whaling, the green dragon's numbers have improved.

Sleeping Pose
Acadian green dragons spend
most of their lives sleeping. This
one held still and ignored our
presence while I drew him.

CHINESE YELLOW DRAGON

BIOLOGY

The Chinese yellow dragon has a unique physiology that distinguishes it from other species within the Dracorexidae family. It is the only member of the great dragons that grows fur like the Arctic dragon family. The Chinese yellow dragon also has five digits on each of its legs instead of four. It has the greatest wingspan of the great dragons, with the fifth of its supra-meta-carpals extended similar to a pterosaur.

Mane and Facial Features
The distinctive mane of the Chinese yellow dragon is thought to be used as a courtship charm. The thick mane, a mixture of fur and elongated scales, grows more ornate and full on the males as they get older. The nasal horn, unique to males, also grows more prominent with age.

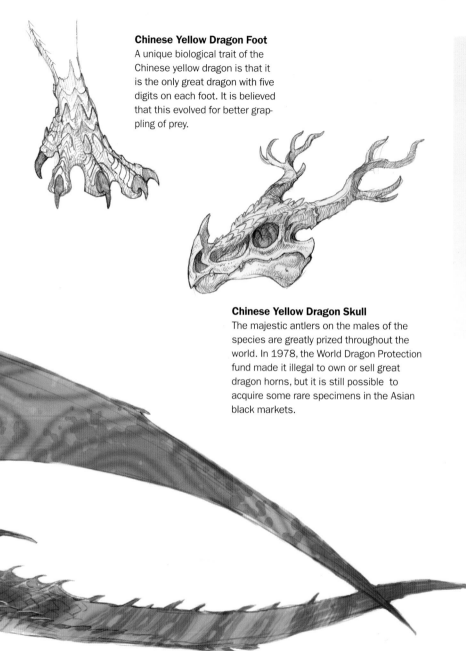

Chinese Yellow Dragon Foot

A unique biological trait of the Chinese yellow dragon is that it is the only great dragon with five digits on each foot. It is believed that this evolved for better grappling of prey.

Chinese Yellow Dragon Skull

The majestic antlers on the males of the species are greatly prized throughout the world. In 1978, the World Dragon Protection fund made it illegal to own or sell great dragon horns, but it is still possible to acquire some rare specimens in the Asian black markets.

SPECIFICATIONS
Dracorexus cathidaeus

Size: 50' (15m)

Wingspan: 100' (30m)

Weight: 10,000 lbs. (4,550kg)

Distribution: East Asia, Yellow Sea

Recognition: Broad narrow wing with only one elongated supra-metacarpal; yellow-gold markings vary by individual and season; ornate antlers and manes on males

Habitat: Mountainous coastal regions

Diet: Fish and cetaceans

Common names: Yellow Dragon, Gold Dragon, Golden Dragon, (Pinyin) Huang Long

Conservation status: Endangered

Chinese Yellow Dragon in Profile, 50' (15m)

Sleek and aerodynamic, the Chinese yellow dragon is famed for its shimmery color and flowing mane.

Chinese Yellow Dragon Egg, 16" (41cm)

Chinese yellow dragon eggs are among the rarest and most valuable due to the dragon's scarcity.

The vast glider-like wings of the Chinese yellow dragon are specifically designed for soaring. Unlike other great dragons that may soar for several hours while hunting for food, the Chinese yellow dragon is known to soar for days, ranging far from its lair in the search for food. Its massive glider wings enable the dragon to achieve astounding altitudes, soaring on the Pacific jet stream as high as 25,000 feet (7,600m) and reaching as far as the Hawaiian Islands.

The primary food source of the Chinese yellow dragon is fish and cetaceans, depending on the size of the individual. Its unique habit is that it can eat its catch while in flight, allowing it to stay out at sea for long periods of time. The Chinese yellow dragon is a nomadic animal, only building a lair or nest when it needs to breed.

BEHAVIOR

Once lush and beautiful, the Bohai Sea is now almost completely dead, destroyed by pollution and overpopulation. With an active oil drilling industry in both the Bohai and Yellow seas adding to the environmental impact, the Chinese yellow dragon's food source has been depleted for nearly 50 years. The Chinese government has been working hard over the past few decades to undo some of the damage. Today, the yellow dragon lives away from the industrial centers of China, Taiwan and Japan and is beginning to gain in numbers, but in the Bohai Straits, Tong Long Huo is the last yellow dragon specimen, protected, fed and cared for by the Chinese government. Tong Long Huo lives at Dragon Rock, where he is visited by millions of tourists a year.

Today, the habitat of this huge animal is scattered due to industrialization, war and the decimation of sea life in its habitat by overfishing and pollution in surrounding waterways. Although the yellow dragon is on the protected list of the World Dragon Protection Fund, it is still actively poached by the Asian black market. The scales, bones, fur, organs and especially the horns of the Chinese yellow dragon are believed to contain powerful medicines to cure everything from arthritis to cancer. The scarcity of the dragon, along with its possession being illegal, makes the Chinese yellow dragon one of the most valuable commodities in the world.

Yellow Dragon Head Variations
There are more than 30 documented species of yellow dragons on the Asian continent and adjoining islands. As you can see from these different heads, yellow dragon depictions vary greatly.

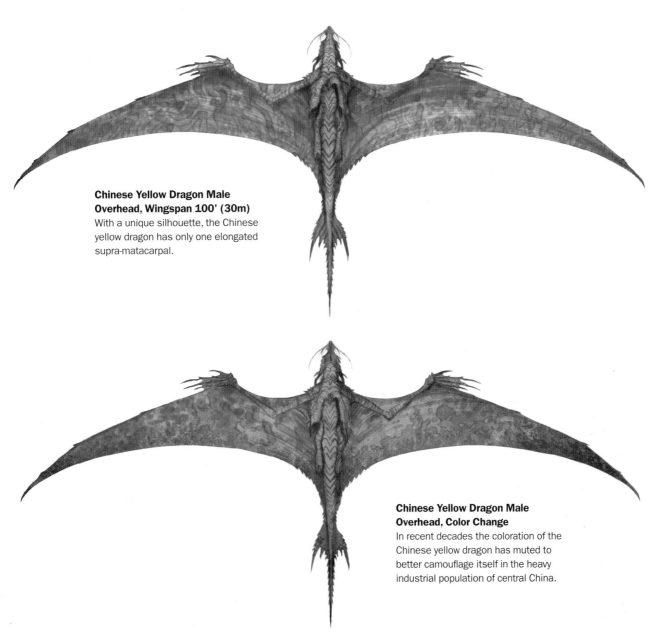

**Chinese Yellow Dragon Male
Overhead, Wingspan 100' (30m)**
With a unique silhouette, the Chinese
yellow dragon has only one elongated
supra-matacarpal.

**Chinese Yellow Dragon Male
Overhead, Color Change**
In recent decades the coloration of the
Chinese yellow dragon has muted to
better camouflage itself in the heavy
industrial population of central China.

HISTORY

The dragons of Asia, and specifically China, have been linked to cultural, national and religious identity since recorded history. Nowhere else in the world is the dragon treated with such universal reverence. In parts of China the people sometimes even refer to themselves as "the descendants of the dragon." In China, the great dragons represent an elemental force of nature most commonly associated with water, the sea and storms. Being so integrally linked to the sea, the yellow dragon is a powerful totem.

Historically there have been many dragons catalogued as Chinese dragons. Although several species of amphiptere, drakes, wyrm and others live within the same habitat, only one species of great dragon lives on the Asian continent. Most often throughout history the Chinese yellow dragon has been misidentified with the Chinese storm dragon and the temple dragon.

CRIMEAN BLACK DRAGON

BIOLOGY

The Crimean black dragon is fairly small compared to some of its great dragon cousins, usually being no more than 25' (8m) long with a 50'(15m) wingspan. There are, however, rumors that during the height of the Cold War, Soviet scientists at the Dracotechnikal Institute bioengineered super-dragons from black dragon stock. Their increased intelligence would allow dragons to fly reconnaissance spy missions over NATO military installations and record data photographically. In 1965, what was believed to be a black dragon was shot down near the Cigli U.S. Air Force Base in Turkey. The Soviet Union has denied any involvement with the incident or that they genetically engineered spy dragons.

**Crimean Black
Dragon Head**

**Crimean Black
Dragon Egg,
2" (5cm)**
These dragon eggs are
very small and tend to
be overlooked.

SPECIFICATIONS
Dracorexus crimeaus

Size: 25' (8m)

Wingspan: 50' (15m)

Weight: 5,000 lbs. (2,270kg)

Distribution: Eastern Europe,
Black Sea

Recognition: Dark black markings; wide tri-forked tail; ridge
spikes; chin prow

Habitat: Coastal regions

Diet: Sturgeon and bass

Common names: Black Dragon,
Czar's Dragon, Russian Dragon,
Apakoh, Onyx Dragon, Scimitar
Dragon

Conservation status: Critically
endangered

Crimean Black Dragon in Profile, 25' (8m)
The Crimean black dragon is distinctive for its
profile. Because of its airplane-like tail, high
dorsal fin, swept wings and pronounced chin
horn, some scientists have suggested that
early Soviet jet airplane designs were modeled
after the Crimean black dragon.

Crimean Black Dragon Hatchling
Born in clutches of one to six eggs, the Crimean dragonling is about
12" (30cm) long when born. The Crimean black dragon is the only
great dragon species to have been successfully bred in captivity.
Today these dragons are raised on a limited scale at the Ukrainian
Dracotechnikal Institute and released into the wild.

Crimean Black Dragon Head
The distinctive profile of the Crimean black dragon's head varies by individual and more greatly between families. Both the male and female possess the pronounced chin prow, although it is more dominant on the males.

Crimean black dragons have survived for millennia off of the plentiful stocks of large Black Sea bass and massive sturgeon in the region's rivers, lakes and seas. It is believed that some examples of Crimean black dragons must have at one time been able to grow twice as big as a specimen today.

BEHAVIOR

The Crimean black dragon was at one time a common sight as far west as the Carpathian Mountains in what is now Romania to the Caucasus in modern-day Turkey and Georgia, making their home along the coasts of the Black and Caspian Seas. Today, however, the best place to see the black dragon is in Crimea along the rocky coasts of the Black Sea.

The majestic Crimean black dragon has become terribly endangered over the past century due to heavy industrialization, diminishing sealife and lack of preservation of their habitat during the Soviet Union's reign. The black dragons in Crimea predominantly lived within the Dracodrome military base in the mountains outside Simferopol. When the Dracodrome was defunded and abandoned in 1991, many of the dragons were destroyed, but some escaped and continue to live within the communities where they had been raised in captivity. Today there are believed to be over two dozen dragons living in the ruins of the former Dracodrome. The area is off limits to outsiders, ostensibly for the safety of the public and the dragon. All attempts by the World Dragon Protection Fund to perform a study of the dragons living at the Dracodrome have been denied by the Ukrainian government.

This tight-knit community of dragons is unique within the Dracorexidae family. Nowhere else in the world are there great dragons living in such close proximity to one another. The highly developed socialization is speculated by some draconologists to be a part of their genetic engineering.

HISTORY

The Crimean peninsula has been one of the most bitterly fought over pieces of geography in history, from the Greeks and Romans to the Ottoman Turks. In 1854, the Crimean War between the Russians and the French ravaged the area, and in World War II, Crimea was sought after by both the Russians and the Germans. Both conflicts devastated most of Crimea. The Crimean peninsula is heavily defunded along its southern coast, which is rimmed with a tall palisade of cliffs near Yalta;

Crimean Liar
Before the 20th century, Crimean black dragons made their lairs in the craggy seashores of the Black, Caspian and Azov Seas and fed upon the giant sturgeon that once populated the waterways. Today Crimean black dragons in the wild are extremely rare as their diet of sturgeon and cetaceans has all but vanished.

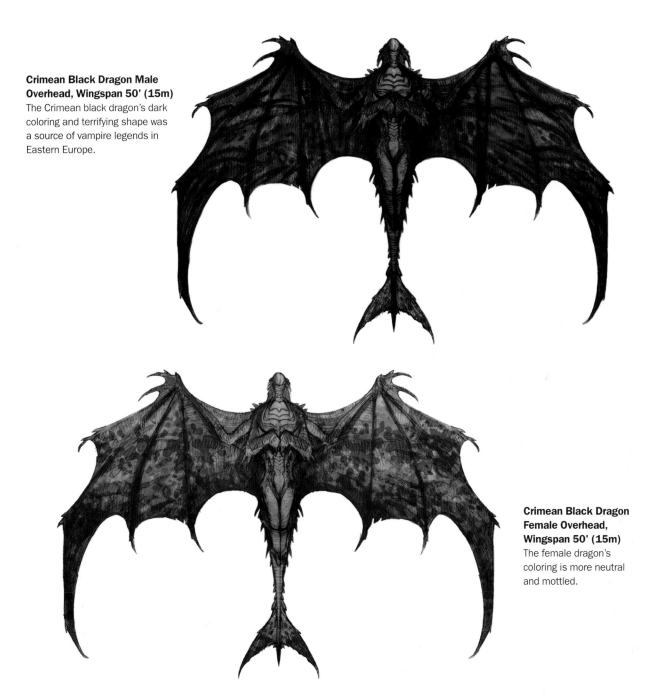

Crimean Black Dragon Male Overhead, Wingspan 50' (15m)
The Crimean black dragon's dark coloring and terrifying shape was a source of vampire legends in Eastern Europe.

Crimean Black Dragon Female Overhead, Wingspan 50' (15m)
The female dragon's coloring is more neutral and mottled.

this has been home to the black dragons for millennia. Because of these repeated military conflicts, as well as massive post-war industrialization and the destruction of most of the fish supply in the Black Sea, the Crimean black dragon has been on the critically endangered list since the 1970s.

Like the Lugrian gray dragon (see page 70), the black dragon has reduced in size in order to survive. In 1941,

during the siege of the Soviet Union in the Battle of the Crimea, Stalin became fascinated with the attempts to genetically engineer animals. The best Soviet draconologists were brought together and commanded to create a weaponized breed of dragons that would be able to intercept Nazi warplanes. Like many of Stalin's eccentric ideas, the creation of a Soviet superdragon was never achieved, but it did serve as a successful propaganda item.

ELWAH BROWN DRAGON

BIOLOGY

The Elwah brown dragon is one of the most distinctive members of the Dracorexidae family. The broad face and short muzzle that give the dragon its uncanny resemblance to an owl has the same function as its avian relative. The broad cone of the dragon's face acts as a sound amplifier focusing subtle noise into the dragon's ear canals. Where most great dragons rely upon sight and smell to hunt, the Elwah brown dragon hunts by sound. The fog-shrouded coasts of the Pacific Northwest make hunting difficult. The dragon uses its high piercing screech to echolocate itself and its relationship to its prey.

BEHAVIOR

The Elwah brown dragon is the newest of the great dragon species to be discovered and studied by western naturalists. This has allowed the brown dragon to remain relatively untouched by human interference for most of its history, creating a very healthy habitat for the animal.

Elwah Brown Dragon Head
The broad head of the Elwah brown dragon has a unique design similar to that of the Strigiformes order of birds commonly known as owls. It helps focus sound.

Elwah Brown Dragon Egg, 12" (30cm)
The surface of an Elwah brown dragon egg is uneven, and the color ranges from spotted to brindle.

SPECIFICATIONS
Dracorexus klallaminus

Size: 50'–75' (15m–23m)

Wingspan: 85' (26m)

Weight: 20,000 lbs. (9,000kg)

Distribution: North American Pacific Northwest

Recognition: Mottled brown and tan markings; broad face with short muzzle; twin forked tail

Habitat: Coastal regions

Diet: Pacific fish, whale

Common names: Brown Dragon, Owl Dragon, Thunderbird, Lightning Serpent, Kuhnuxwah, Webber's Dragon, Salish Dragon

Conservation status: Vulnerable

Elwah Brown Dragon in Profile, 75' (23m)
The short, beak-like snout of the Elwah brown dragon allows it to hunt by sound far better than by sight.

Elwah Brown Dragon Hatchlings
A clutch of Elwah brown dragon eggs usually consists of 2 to 6 hatchlings.

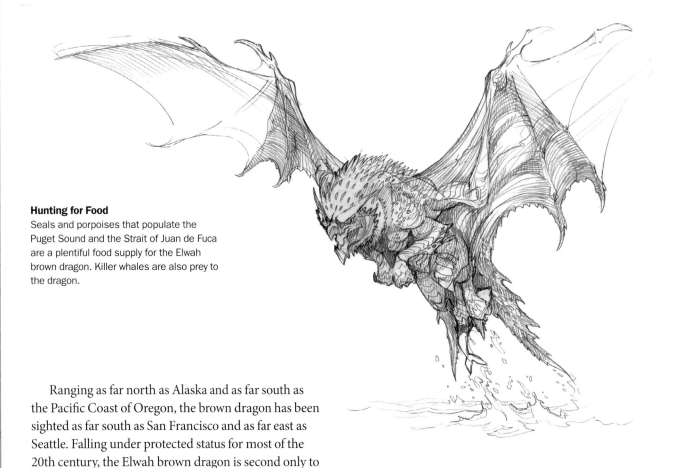

Hunting for Food
Seals and porpoises that populate the Puget Sound and the Strait of Juan de Fuca are a plentiful food supply for the Elwah brown dragon. Killer whales are also prey to the dragon.

Ranging as far north as Alaska and as far south as the Pacific Coast of Oregon, the brown dragon has been sighted as far south as San Francisco and as far east as Seattle. Falling under protected status for most of the 20th century, the Elwah brown dragon is second only to the Icelandic white dragon (see chapter 5) in population. It is believed that over 5,000 Elwah brown dragons are alive today, living off the abundant food supplies of the Pacific fish and whale populations.

HISTORY

Although the Elwah brown dragon has been known by the Native American tribes of the Pacific Northwest for millennia, the first European account of this dragon took place in 1778. Captain Cook's third circumnavigation of the world brought his ship, the *HMS Resolution*, to Vancouver Island for over a month that year. The ship's artist, John Webber, documented the dragon for the National Society of London for Improving Natural Knowledge. This encounter gave the dragon its first moniker, Webber's dragon.

In 1805, Lewis and Clark arrived in the Pacific Northwest. It was from the accounts of this expedition that the dragon was officially classified as "Elwah" in 1823. Early naturalists learned that the dragon was referred to by Native American tribes as "the thunderbird" and played an important role in their spiritual celebrations. The

Elwah Brown Dragon Nest
The Elwah brown dragon is a social animal. Like its avian cousins, it will care for its young until they are old enough to leave the lair. Here a male has brought a harbor seal to a dragonling born earlier in the spring.

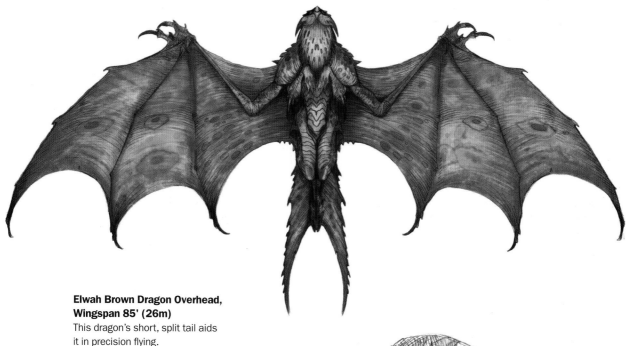

**Elwah Brown Dragon Overhead,
Wingspan 85' (26m)**
This dragon's short, split tail aids
it in precision flying.

thunderbird represents the awesome power
of nature and a respect for life. Referred to as a
Kuhnuxwah in some Pacific Northwest languages,
the dragon was able to shape-shift into human form.

The relative isolation and abundance of the
Elwah brown dragon made the great beast
a favorite for American and European sport
hunters. In 1909, former president Theodore
Roosevelt shot three brown dragons during an
expedition to the region. The president was an
ardent supporter of the Elwah National Dragon
Sanctuary, which was dedicated in 1917.

In 1923, the Canadian government created
the Canadian National Elwah Preserve,
and today the International Elwah Dragon
Sanctuary is the only international dragon
preserve. In 1982, the Elwah National Dragon
Sanctuary's control was transferred to the
Elwah Tribal Council, making it the only
national park under the jurisdiction of a
Native American tribe.

Elwah Brown Dragon Lair
A guide inspects a vacant
dragon lair.

ICELANDIC WHITE DRAGON

BIOLOGY

Ranging as far north as Greenland, as far west as Prince Edward Island, Canada, and as far southeast as the Orkney Islands in Scotland, the Icelandic white dragon has been known to come into contact with the Acadian, Welsh and Scandinavian dragons.

BEHAVIOR

Unlike most other great dragons of the world, the Icelandic white dragon is so prolific that competition for premium nesting grounds is fierce. Males often spar in the spring using their horns as weapons to duel for a coveted nesting spot. The combat can become fierce and the scars from combat are evidenced on many of the older bulls. Once a proper nesting spot or lair has been established, the Icelandic white dragon builds a nest and tries to attract a female with his prominent displays of fire, colorful neck wattle and sonorous dragon song.

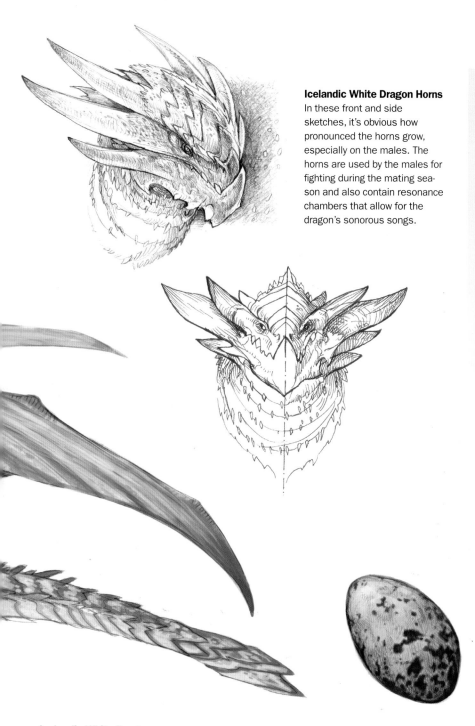

Icelandic White Dragon Horns
In these front and side sketches, it's obvious how pronounced the horns grow, especially on the males. The horns are used by the males for fighting during the mating season and also contain resonance chambers that allow for the dragon's sonorous songs.

SPECIFICATIONS
Dracorexus reykjavikus

Size: 50'–75' (15m–23m)

Wingspan: 85' (26m)

Weight: 20,000 lbs. (9,000kg)

Distribution: North Atlantic

Recognition: Markings range from pure white to mottled brown, depending on the season; broad horizontal cranial horns; delta wings; pronounced upward beak; females duller and more mottled in color

Habitat: Coastal regions

Diet: Fish, cetaceans, whales

Common names: White Dragon, Polar Dragon

Conservation status: Near threatened

Icelandic White Dragon in Profile, 75' (23m)
This powerful, resilient dragon is a fierce fighter and highly territorial.

Icelandic White Dragon Egg, 16" (41cm)
Sketched from a sample at the Icelandic Museum of Natural History. The egg of the Icelandic white dragon may sit dormant for years before hatching. A female will guard the nest for as long as necessary. The eggs of the Icelandic white dragon can hibernate in a deep freeze if weather conditions grow too cold.

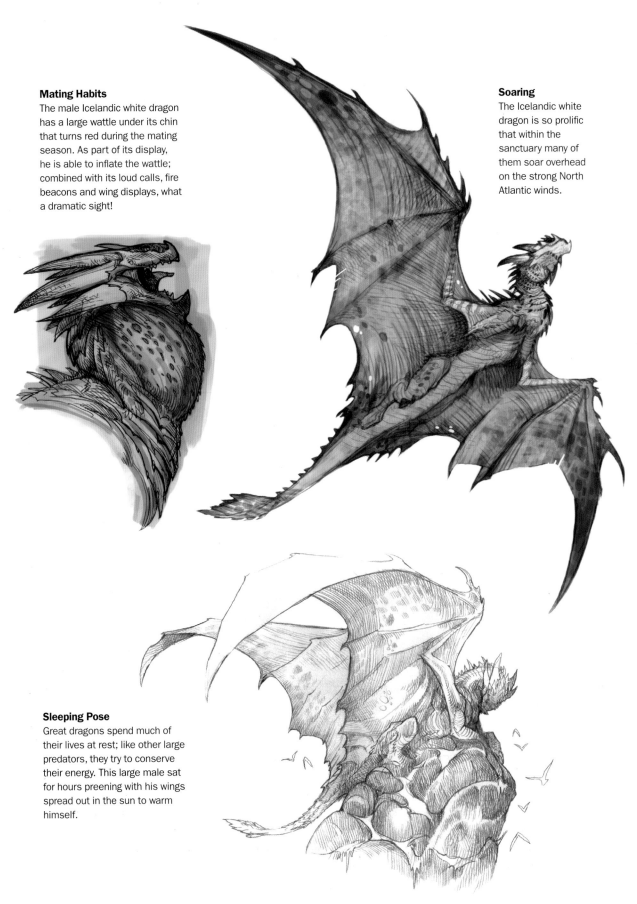

Mating Habits

The male Icelandic white dragon has a large wattle under its chin that turns red during the mating season. As part of its display, he is able to inflate the wattle; combined with its loud calls, fire beacons and wing displays, what a dramatic sight!

Soaring

The Icelandic white dragon is so prolific that within the sanctuary many of them soar overhead on the strong North Atlantic winds.

Sleeping Pose

Great dragons spend much of their lives at rest; like other large predators, they try to conserve their energy. This large male sat for hours preening with his wings spread out in the sun to warm himself.

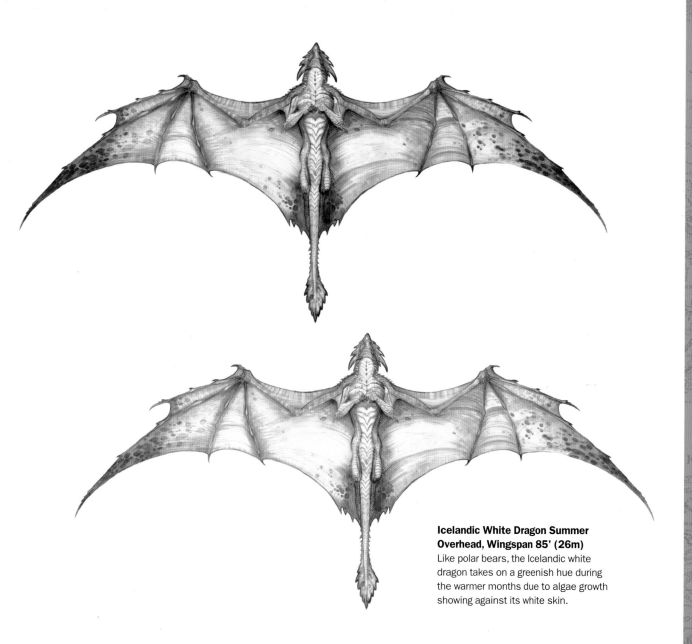

Icelandic White Dragon Summer Overhead, Wingspan 85' (26m)
Like polar bears, the Icelandic white dragon takes on a greenish hue during the warmer months due to algae growth showing against its white skin.

Depending upon its size, the white dragon commonly hunts the fish and cetaceans surrounding its habitat. When the dragons are young, North Atlantic tuna is a common fish food. When grown to maturity, the Icelandic white dragon is able to hunt large sea mammals such as killer whales and juvenile humpback, fin and right whales.

HISTORY

The Icelandic white dragon is one of the most famous and abundant dragons in history. At the height of its growth the range of the Icelandic white dragon must have exceeded its own food supply. By the early medieval period, there were reports of the Icelandic white dragon coming within the range of the Scandinavian blue and the Welsh red dragons of Europe. The most famous account is in the medieval Welsh epic the *Mabinogion*. In the story, a white dragon attacks a red dragon in Britain. In the end both dragons are subdued by King Lludd. It is remarkable that Icelandic white dragons may have ranged as far east and south as Wales over 500 years ago, indicating just how prolific they must have been. Over the subsequent centuries of Iceland's colonization, the dragon numbers have diminished, but they are still the largest population of the great dragon species.

LIGURIAN GRAY DRAGON

BIOLOGY

The Ligurian gray dragon is not only the rarest but also the most biologically different of the great dragons. It is also the only dragon species that has more than five supra-metacarpals in its wings. A total of ten metacarpal bones radiate out from the radius and ulna bones. This unique construction makes for dexterous movements of the wings, allowing the dragons great maneuverability in the air. Biologists have debated over the past few centuries whether to include the Ligurian gray dragon within the family Dracorexidae, or to devote it to a whole new family. The Ligurian gray dragon also has the distinction of being the smallest of the great dragons with a maximum recorded wingspan of only 25' (8m), and an average wingspan of about 15' (5m). It is often mistaken for the amphiptere species that live in the Cinque Terre region. The Ligurian gray dragon is the southernmost species of great dragons.

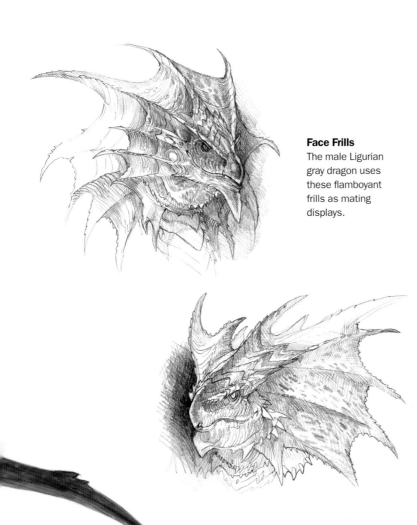

Face Frills
The male Ligurian gray dragon uses these flamboyant frills as mating displays.

SPECIFICATIONS
Dracorexus cinqaterrus

Size: 15' (5m)

Wingspan: 25' (8m)

Weight: 2,500 lbs. (1,135kg)

Distribution: Northern Italy

Recognition: Gray-silver markings on males with bright lavender-violet during mating season; subtler colors on females; ten-digit wings; large crests and frills along neck and tail

Habitat: Coastal regions

Diet: Cetaceans

Common names: Dragoni, Dragonara, Dracogrigio, Silver Dragon, Amethyst Dragon

Conservation status: Highly endangered

Ligurian Gray Dragon Egg, 6" (15cm)
Environmental changes have made the Ligurian gray dragon very rare. It is believed there may be as few as a dozen mating pairs left in the wild. The eggs of the Ligurian gray dragon are a national treasure handled with the same care as the master artworks of the nation.

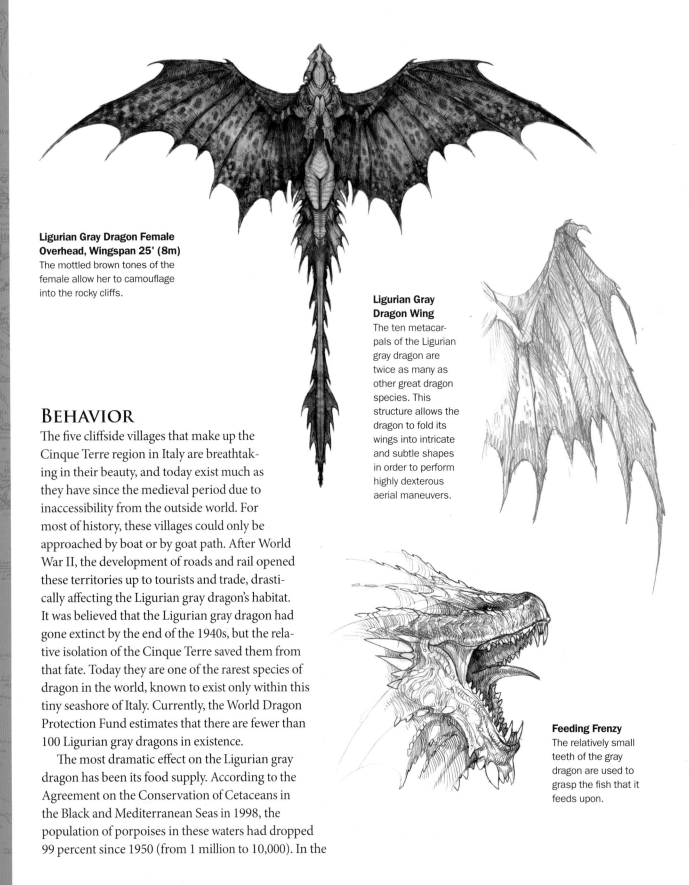

Ligurian Gray Dragon Female Overhead, Wingspan 25' (8m)
The mottled brown tones of the female allow her to camouflage into the rocky cliffs.

Ligurian Gray Dragon Wing
The ten metacarpals of the Ligurian gray dragon are twice as many as other great dragon species. This structure allows the dragon to fold its wings into intricate and subtle shapes in order to perform highly dexterous aerial maneuvers.

Feeding Frenzy
The relatively small teeth of the gray dragon are used to grasp the fish that it feeds upon.

Behavior

The five cliffside villages that make up the Cinque Terre region in Italy are breathtaking in their beauty, and today exist much as they have since the medieval period due to inaccessibility from the outside world. For most of history, these villages could only be approached by boat or by goat path. After World War II, the development of roads and rail opened these territories up to tourists and trade, drastically affecting the Ligurian gray dragon's habitat. It was believed that the Ligurian gray dragon had gone extinct by the end of the 1940s, but the relative isolation of the Cinque Terre saved them from that fate. Today they are one of the rarest species of dragon in the world, known to exist only within this tiny seashore of Italy. Currently, the World Dragon Protection Fund estimates that there are fewer than 100 Ligurian gray dragons in existence.

The most dramatic effect on the Ligurian gray dragon has been its food supply. According to the Agreement on the Conservation of Cetaceans in the Black and Mediterranean Seas in 1998, the population of porpoises in these waters had dropped 99 percent since 1950 (from 1 million to 10,000). In the

**Ligurian Gray Dragon Male
Overhead, Wingspan 25' (8m)**
The coloring on the male ranges
from pale silver to vibrant purple.

late 20th century, drastic measures were taken
to protect cetaceans living in the Mediterranean.
These efforts have helped to save the Ligurian
gray dragon from extinction, but it is still acutely
threatened despite living in one of the most envi-
ronmentally protected regions in the world.

History

Based upon documents from earlier studies and depictions in scientific journals from as early as the 17th
century, it is believed that the Ligurian gray dragon has
shrunk in size almost 30 percent. With the depletion
of marine mammals, the gray has needed to change its
feeding habits from porpoises and seals to tuna and sea
bass. The larger specimens very likely starved to death,
leaving a smaller breeding population.

The Cinque Terra region in northern Italy comprises
all that is left of the Ligurian gray dragon's habitat and
exists uniquely as a region where dragons and humans
can live in the closest proximity to one another. The
Ligurian people and government take great pride in this
fact. Most of the depictions of dragons created during
the Italian Renaissance and Baroque periods are of gray
dragons.

Sunbathing Gray Dragon
The Mediterranean sun helps
the dragons warm themselves.

73

SCANDINAVIAN BLUE DRAGON

BIOLOGY

The Scandinavian blue dragon is a broad-ranging species known to make lairs as far south as Scotland, east into Russia, and even as far west as the Faroe Islands. The plentiful populations of seals, porpoises and whales in these areas provide ample food, allowing blue dragons to thrive along the sparsely inhabited, rugged coasts of Scandinavia.

The Scandinavian blue dragon nests and lives along the rocky coasts of the Scandinavian peninsula, which includes Norway, Sweden, Denmark and Finland. The adequate rainfall, mild temperatures, high rugged cliffs overlooking the Norwegian Sea, fjords brimming with whales and cetaceans, and sparse human populations make this region the healthiest dragon habitat in the

Scandinavian Blue Dragon in Profile, 75' (23m)
During mating season, the Scandinavian blue male displays its vibrant colors to attract a mate.

Size: 50'–100' (15m–30m)

Wingspan: 75'–85' (23m–26m)

Weight: 20,000 lbs. (9,000kg)

Distribution: Northern Europe

Recognition: Bright blue markings on males (subtler on females); elongated snout; paddle rudder on tail; canard wing behind hip

Habitat: Coastal regions

Diet: Porpoises, whales, seals

Common names: Nordic Dragon, Blue Dragon, Norwegian Dragon, Fjord Wyrm

Conservation status: Vulnerable

Color Variations
The famous blue dragon of Norway is not always blue. The Scandinavian dragon possesses the widest range of coloring among individuals and regions, even changing throughout the seasons. Patterns and colors on these males make identification easier for scientists.

Eating Habits
The long snout of the Scandinavian blue dragon allows it to open its mouth wide, enabling it to swallow fish whole.

Scandinavian Blue Dragon Egg, 18" (46cm)
The eggs of Scandinavian dragons are camouflaged to blend in with the blue granite of the fjords.

world. Although the Scandinavian blue dragon's range is not as large as the Icelandic white's, there are more great dragons living along the fjords of Norway than anywhere else in the world.

The stunning habitat of the Scandinavian blue dragon makes Norway one of the most popular dragon destinations in the world. One way to tour the visual splendor of Norway is the Dragon-Fjord Cruiseline, one of the most successful businesses in the country. To protect its habitat for the future from both hunting and the impact of environmental tourism, the Norwegian government has dedicated several nature preserves along the southeastern coasts and fjords as dragon preserves.

Behavior

Similar to other species of great dragons, the Scandinavian blue dragon requires a wide hunting range, isolated windswept peaks and plentiful waters to provide enough food to sustain the larger specimens of the species.

A mature male Scandinavian dragon can weigh more than 10 tons (9,089kg), its wingspan can reach up to 100 feet (30m) and it can consume nearly 150 lbs. (68kg) of meat per day. The Scandinavian, like all great dragons, has long periods of metabolic stasis and hibernation, requiring the hunting of food only about once a week in the summer and once a month in the winter. Older individuals may eat only once a month in summer and sleep through the whole winter. Plentiful supplies of cetaceans in the waters off the Norwegian coast allow the dragons to hunt infrequently, catching large marine mammals that they will take back to their lairs to feed on.

The Scandinavian blue dragon also hunts large food fish such as North Atlantic tuna and smaller cetaceans such as pilot and killer whales, so they do not interfere with the fishing trade, which mostly nets smaller food fish like herring. The extinction of the European wyvern in the late 19th century, combined with whale hunting controls in the late 20th century, has helped to dramatically increase the number of Scandinavian blue dragons. As such, they have the highest conservation rating of any great dragon.

Hunting
Soaring high over the North Atlantic coast of Norway, the Scandinavian blue dragon can glide for hours searching the ocean for pods of whales and schools of fish.

Scandinavian Blue Dragon Hatchling

History

The Scandinavian blue dragon has not posed much of a threat to humans despite living in close proximity for centuries. The dragon has been regarded by Scandinavian cultures as a creature of great magic and power and was particularly revered by early Nordic and Viking cultures. We visited the very impressive Hall of Dragons, a collection of dragon artifacts at the Bergen Academy of Natural Sciences. The Scandinavian people have revered and studied the dragon for centuries.

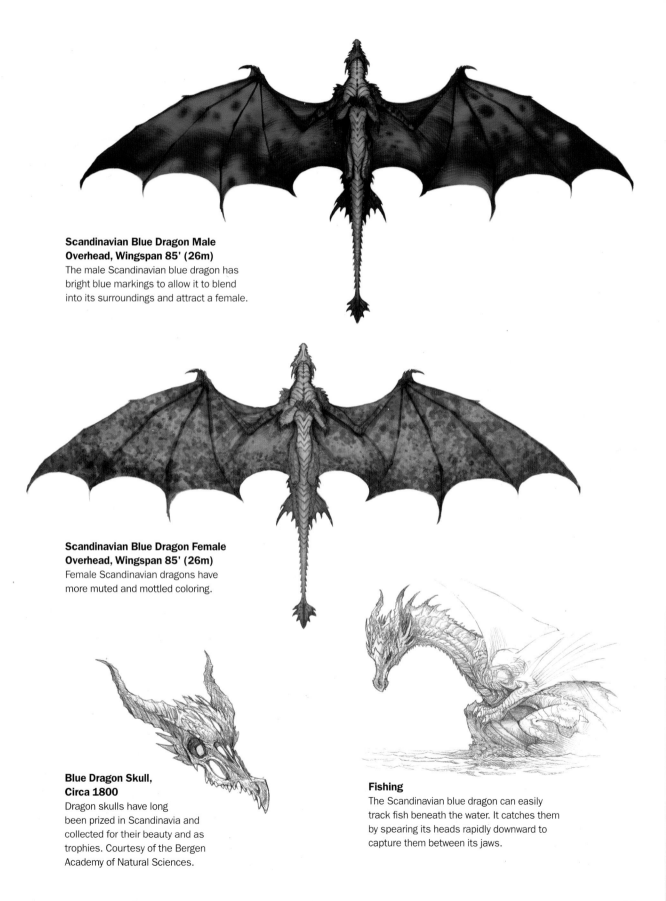

**Scandinavian Blue Dragon Male
Overhead, Wingspan 85' (26m)**
The male Scandinavian blue dragon has
bright blue markings to allow it to blend
into its surroundings and attract a female.

**Scandinavian Blue Dragon Female
Overhead, Wingspan 85' (26m)**
Female Scandinavian dragons have
more muted and mottled coloring.

**Blue Dragon Skull,
Circa 1800**
Dragon skulls have long
been prized in Scandinavia and
collected for their beauty and as
trophies. Courtesy of the Bergen
Academy of Natural Sciences.

Fishing
The Scandinavian blue dragon can easily
track fish beneath the water. It catches them
by spearing its heads rapidly downward to
capture them between its jaws.

WELSH RED DRAGON

BIOLOGY

While it is true that the Welsh red is the rarest of the western dragons, its protected status for hundreds of years under the protection of the royal crown has allowed the animal to survive.

Like other great dragons, the female red mates only once every few years and her gestation period is extensive, sometimes lasting up to 36 months. A clutch usually consists of only three eggs, which are fiercely guarded by both the mother and father. When the hatchlings are born, they are no more than the size of a puppy, requiring great attention for several years until they can fend for themselves. During this time period the male

Welsh Red Dragon in Profile, 75' (23m)

SPECIFICATIONS
Dracorexus idraigoxus

Size: 75' (23m)

Wingspan: 100' (30m)

Weight: 30,000 lbs. (1,3620kg)

Distribution: Northern Britain

Recognition: Bright red markings on males (subtler on females); nasal and chin horn on males; paddle rudder on tail; canard wings behind hip

Habitat: Coastal regions

Diet: Fish, whales

Common names: Draig, Red Dragon, Red Wyrm

Conservation status: Endangered

Color Variations
Like other dragons, the Welsh red dragon has a wide variation of patterns and colors between male and female. The frills and horns of the male are absent in the female, as are the bright markings that become deeper in the fall.

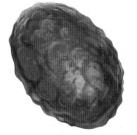

Welsh Red Dragon Egg, 17" (43cm)
The Welsh red dragon egg has an unusually rough surface and stony texture.

**Welsh Red Dragon Male Overhead,
Wingspan 100' (30m)**
The enormous wingspans of the adult
Welsh red dragon make them truly
wondrous to watch in flight.

BEHAVIOR

The great Welsh red dragon of folklore and history is
by far the most famous within the *Dracorexidae* family
of dragons. Although the red dragons do not have as
large a range as the Icelandic white and Scandinavian
blue dragons and are far rarer (estimated fewer than
200 remaining), they hold the distinctions of living in
such close connection to the humans in their area that
the relationship is almost symbiotic. Dragon-human
contact, however, is almost unheard of.

The current range of the Welsh red dragon stretches
north to the Faroe Islands, south into Wales, and across
much of the northern islands of Scotland, where the
dragons hunt seals and small whales from the sea.

HISTORY

Perhaps nowhere else in the world is the land so inter-
twined with its dragons as in Wales. Wales is synonymous with dragons, and the Welsh red dragon is
emblazoned on their flag and woven into their national
mythology. The dragons had very little contact with
humans until the English settlement of Wales in the
Medieval period.

Red dragons have been historically well protected
in Wales. Technically all red dragons are protected as
the personal stock of the royal family dating back to the
reign of King Edward I. It was this aristocratic land

usually does all the hunting of fish and whales, bringing
the kill back to the lair where the female protects her
young. Once the hatchlings have learned to fly, the males
leave the lair and begin looking for a new territory.

Due to disease, perdition or accident, only approxi-
mately 20 percent of Welsh red dragon hatchlings
survive to adulthood, which means that one Welsh red
dragon couple may produce only a single adult dragon
on average once every twenty years. Through conservation and preservation these numbers are improving, but
the Welsh red dragon remains squarely on the endangered species list.

Welsh Red Dragon Female Overhead, Wingspan 100' (30m)
The female dragons have softer, earthier colors that help them blend into their natural surroundings.

management and strict protection that allowed the Welsh dragon to survive well into the 21st century while other dragon species like the European wyvern and the lindworm were hunted to extinction.

For centuries the royalty of Britain regularly hunted dragons in royal game forests like Trenadog Royal Dragon Trust, maintained by the famous Welsh dragon ghillies. The last red dragon hunt to take place was in 1907. Today the dragon ghillies act as guides for naturalists and visitors. Although it is illegal to hunt the red dragon, a dragon ghillie may use force if a dragon threatens humans or their homes, but this is a rare occurrence.

Common Drake
Pencil and digital
14" × 22" (36cm × 56cm)

DRAKE

Draco drakidae

BIOLOGY

The drake is a common flightless dragon that was domesticated early by many civilizations. The drake comes in hundreds of species and breeds, but all are four-legged animals with short compact bodies allowing for swift running. The great advantage to the drake is its ability to adapt to its environment and create hundreds of subspecies that are specially designed for almost any function. The drake's powerful jaws and sharp teeth are evolved to effectively capture and kill its prey.

BEHAVIOR

Drakes are naturally a pack hunting animal living in the grasslands and open savannahs around the world and as far north as subarctic tundra. Groups of drakes can grow to several dozen bringing down large game such as elk, moose and dragonettes. Today there are very few wild species of drake in the world having been hunted to near extinction.

Wedge-Shaped Head of the Common Drake
The wedge-shaped head allows for binocular vision when hunting. Powerful jaws and dragon beak are utilized to kill its prey.

Drake Habitat
Drakes thrive in a variety of climates and terrain, especially the grasslands and open savannahs of the world, where they can take advantage of their natural speed.

Warrior's Ally
For centuries drakes have been used as hunting animals and as guards. Custom armor and harnesses have been developed for their varied occupations.

Drake Egg, 10" (25cm)
In the wild, drakes live in packs, which guard the nests from scavengers.

History

Originally domesticated by the Egyptian and Babylonian cultures, the wild drake no longer exists in the numbers they used to. Bred throughout the world, hundreds of varieties of drake have been developed over the centuries from small toy drakes no more than 12" (30cm) long, to the massive siege drake over 20' (6m) long. In North America and Europe the wild species of drake have been hunted to near extinction up into the mid-20th century when they were placed on the endangered species list. Modern sanctuaries, parks and preserves have seen numbers of wild drakes on the rise.

Because of their common usage as guard animals, drakes in art routinely graced architecture from Mesopotamia, Egypt and Asia. During the Middle Ages the drake became such a symbol of protection and ferocity that their likeness was used on cathedrals and churches as downspouts and to help deter nesting pigeons. These "gurglers" became known as gargoyles and today the term is synonymous with the drake in many parts of the world.

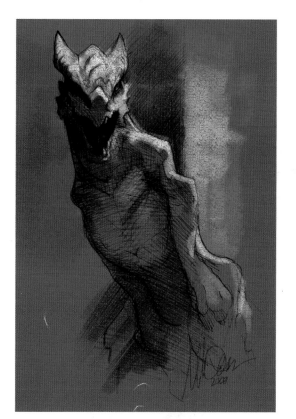

Gargoyles
Used as waterspouts on Gothic cathedrals in Europe, these stone carvings, or gargoyles, depict dragons of all types, but drakes are the most common.

COMMON DRAKE

The common drake has been found all over the world and, therefore, has been one of the easiest drake species to acquire for domestication. This drake's swift speed and powerful musculature make it ideal for hunting and military purposes.

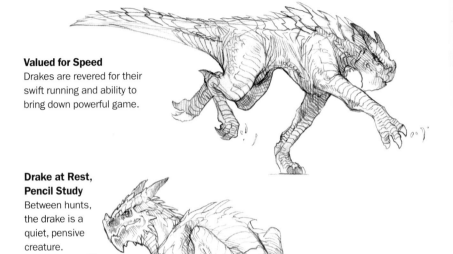

Valued for Speed
Drakes are revered for their swift running and ability to bring down powerful game.

Drake at Rest, Pencil Study
Between hunts, the drake is a quiet, pensive creature.

Drake Skull
The skull of the drake has large areas for the attachment of jaw muscles and ligaments for their powerful bite.

SPECIFICATIONS
Drakus plebeius

Size: 3'–12' (91cm–4m)

Distribution: Worldwide

Recognition: Quadrupedal stocky body; flightless

Habitat: Temperate to tropical climates and open plains

Diet: Elk, moose, dragonflies

Common names: Gargoyle, Drakoyle, Gorgon, Draggonne, Drak

Conservation status: Least concern

St. Cuthbert's Drake

This drake was domesticated in the Middle Ages by the monks of St. Cuthbert's Abbey in Bavaria. Its sturdy build allowed it to climb rocky landscapes to aid pilgrims lost in the snow. Scarce today, the St. Cuthbert's drake is still respected for its sheer power, and it is occasionally put to work for agricultural purposes.

SPECIFICATIONS
Drakus eruous

Size: 10' (3m)

Distribution: Worldwide

Recognition: High, powerful front shoulder

Habitat: Rocky, mountainous environments

Diet: Mammals, birds, grasses

Common names: Mountain Bull, Udo's Ox

Conservation Status: Scarce

St. George's Drake

St. George's drake is one of the most adaptable members of the drake family. It is found in varied climates and a variety of environments. Its uncommon status, however, makes it unusual to find domesticated in human settlements.

SPECIFICATIONS
Drakus imperatorus

Size: 14' (4m)

Distribution: Worldwide

Recognition: Small, even spikes along the spinal ridge and short nasal horn

Habitat: Grasslands, open plains, dry climates

Diet: Small mammals, rodents, reptiles

Common names: Comb Back, Desert Gator

Conservation Status: Uncommon

PIT DRAKE

While many drakes have been bred for fighting, the pit drake is the most notorious. It is illegal to breed pit drakes in many countries. Although known as a formidable fighter since Roman times because of its size and power, the breed is not aggressive by nature and these creatures make loyal companions.

SPECIFICATIONS
Drakus barathrumus

Size: 4' (122cm)

Distribution: Worldwide

Recognition: Squat stature, powerful build

Habitat: Marshlands

Diet: Amphibians, snakes, birds

Common names: Pittraggo, Arena Dragon, Carnethus

Conservation status: Uncommon

PYLE'S DRAKE

Various subspecies of Pyle's drake can be found on both sides of the Atlantic in moderate climates. Originally found in North America, it was later brought to the Mediterranean region. Pyle's drake is a digger and has been used throughout history to hunt burrowing mammals, from rats to wolverines.

SPECIFICATIONS
Drakus gargoylius

Size: 500' (152m)

Distribution: Atlantic basin

Recognition: High, arching, spiked back; dual, front-facing horns; usually striped

Habitat: Grasslands

Diet: Mammals, rodents, reptiles

Common names: Toro Drake, Horned Howard, Rehoboth Ram

Conservation status: Scarce

ISHTAR DRAKE

The earliest known domesticated drake is the Ishtar drake, now extinct. This reconstruction is based on the depiction of the same animal on the Ishtar Gate in Baghdad, Iraq, the oldest known depiction of any dragon in history (ca. 3000 B.C.). Remains of a similar species have been found mummified with pharaohs in Egypt. It is believed that all contemporary drakes stem from this one ancestor.

SPECIFICATIONS
Drakus ishtarus

Size: 6' (2m)

Distribution: Northern Africa, Arabian peninsula and the Middle East

Recognition: Slender racing form with elongated neck

Habitat: Wetlands and riverbanks

Diet: Fish, crocodiles, birds

Common name: Godstreak

Conservation status: Extinct

WYETH'S DRAKE

First reported in the logbooks of early mapping expeditions, the Wyeth's drake was among the first of the New World drakes encountered by explorers. Not a common animal then, they became the subject of early hunting by Western settlers. Their numbers have been reduced to dangerously low levels, leaving them protected in some countries, and all but entirely absent in others.

SPECIFICATIONS
Dracus brandywinus

Size: 7' (2m)

Distribution: Central and South America

Recognition: Large nasal horn, uneven spinal ridge

Habitat: Marsh, brackish water inlets

Diet: Fish, mammals, reptiles

Common name: Umber Drake

Conservation status: Critically endangered

SIEGE DRAKE

RACING DRAKE

Large drakes like the siege drake were bred until the 19th century for use in warfare. They often pulled chariots and cannons, and they were occasionally used to carry the bodies of injured soldiers off the battlefield.

SPECIFICATIONS
Drakus bellumus

Size: 16' (5m)

Distribution: Eurasia, northwest North America

Recognition: Short neck; large body; four developed spikes that grow opposite the limbs

Habitat: Rocky, arid terrain

Diet: Small mammals

Common names: Battle Drake, Kriegsdrakkon

Conservation Status: Scarce

Small, swift racing drakes are still bred today. Their speeds can rival those of a cheetah, which makes for entertaining events when raced competitively. This has been done with marked success in many cultures, though recent steps to ensure the safety of the animals have revealed numerous endangerments, and the practice of competitive racing has lessened considerably.

SPECIFICATIONS
Drakus properitus

Size: 6' (2m)

Distribution: Asia, Australia, Africa

Recognition: Long legs with elevated hindquarters; minimal spinal ridge; beaklike jaw

Habitat: Dry grasslands

Diet: Scavenged meat

Common name: Swift

Conservation Status: Uncommon

Hydra
Pencil and digital
14" × 22" (36cm × 56cm)

HYDRA

Draco hydridae

BIOLOGY

By far the most unusual family in the Draconia class, the hydra is an order of dragon consisting of families and species that possess multiple serpentine necks and heads known as Hydradraciformes. The hydra is born with only two heads, and as the creature grows in size, it sprouts new heads that allow it to feed more effectively. If heads are damaged or destroyed, new heads are capable of growing back. The image of heads sprouting back like magic is an exaggeration; rather, a new hydra head usually takes one year to grow in. The hydra's habitat is located around bodies of water, where its many heads are used to hunt fish and small game.

Head of the Hydra
The hydra lives in deep murky swamps and has terrible eyesight. It often hunts at night in order to catch its prey. The head is equipped with long tendril-like whiskers that it uses to sense the environment around it.

Hydra Habitat
Most commonly found making its dens near large rivers around the world, the hydra has become an endangered creature as much of its habitat has been destroyed by development of human settlements, and the construction of dams.

Hydra Egg, 10" (25cm)
Hydra do not care for their young. They lay a small clutch of eggs and abandon them to their fate. Hydra hatchlings will often kill one another looking for food. This harsh parenting and childhood accounts for the scarcity of hydra.

The Lernaen hydra is much smaller, only 10'–20' (3m–6m). It has a serpentine body, no legs, and is often referred to as a wyrm (see chapter 10), but it is actually in the Hydridae family.

Both the Indian hydra, or naga, and the Japanese hydra, or Yamato no Orochi, live by the sea, hunting shellfish in saltwater tidal flats and up rivers.

The cerebrus hydra is a smaller species, usually confused with a drake (see chapter 6) or even a canine, but it is, in fact, a hydra. The cerebrus is unique in that it is born with three heads and is unable to grow new ones. It hunts small game in open grasslands and is often captured to be used as a guard animal, often tethered near a portal or gate. Its three heads are always alert, and unlike the other hydra species, it is able to growl and bark like a hound to alert its keepers.

The aero hydra, or winged hydra, has never been documented and it is considered unlikely that such an ungainly creature could ever function in the air. Yet, hydra specialists are constantly on the lookout for the elusive winged hydra.

BEHAVIOR

Hunted with extreme prejudice since ancient times to protect people and livestock, the hydra has disappeared from its classical habitats such as the Nile Delta and the Mediterranean islands. Larger specimens are known to attack livestock, but usually the hydra is an angler, hunting easy prey that comes within the grasp of its tentacle-like necks. The large, bulky body is armored to protect against other predators such as crocodiles, but this makes the hydra a ponderous animal that may not move from its lair for weeks.

The hydra is notoriously unintelligent, with the individual brains of each head minuscule in comparison to its body size. The heads are capable of autonomous actions, allowing some heads to rest while others continue feeding.

The hydra will attack anything that moves within the path of its heads as it lays in wait along riverbanks and inland seas. It has been observed that hydra heads will often fight one another, resulting in injury or the death of one of the heads.

In the winter months the northern bull hydra will burrow underground and hibernate, while the subtropical and tropical Lernaen hydra, naga and Japanese hydra remain active year round.

HISTORY

The hydra is one of the most commonly depicted dragons in art history and is ubiquitous in almost all cultures. The hydra has been depicted thousands of times in Grecian urns, classical mosaics, Islamic scrolls and sculpture, Buddhist murals, and medieval illuminated manuscripts, paintings and engravings. The Lernaen hydra is most famous for its classical battle against Hercules, but there are other accounts of multiheaded dragons. In Japanese mythology, the sea god Susanoo battles an eight-headed hydra by getting it drunk on sake. In India, the god Vishnu dances on the head of a naga. In the Christian faith, the famous seven-headed beast of the apocalypse is assumed to be inspired by the European bull hydra.

Hydra Feet
The soft, muddy ground of the hydra's habitat requires a broad, flat webbed foot to support the creature's bulky weight.

EUROPEAN BULL HYDRA

The European bull is the best-known hydra in Western culture. Its large size, numerous heads and unpredictable nature make it a formidable foe, featured in many heroic tales. Remains of these great beasts rarely survive a generation because of the fragile nature of their bone structures. Their legends live on in art and stories.

SPECIFICATIONS
Hydridae rhonus

Size: 30' (9m)

Distribution: Europe, Middle East, Central Asia

Recognition: Serpentine body with multiple heads

Habitat: Temperate to tropical climate, waterways and wetlands

Diet: Fish, small game

Common names: Rhone Hydra, Star Dragon

Conservation status: Extinct

Swimming Hydra

Despite being ungainly on land, hydra are excellent swimmers. Moving around their territory requires frequent river crossings. The hollow bones common to all dragons make them extremely buoyant.

Japanese Hydra

The Japanese hydra (or Yamato no Orochi) is the rarest of all the hydra species, having once thrived along the riverbanks and streams of the southern islands of Japan, Okinawa and South Korea. The timorous dragon makes its home lurking along riverbeds and hiding under rocks and logs near streams, using its multiple heads to catch small fry and insects along the riverbank. Larger specimen can catch birds, small fish, reptiles and even small mammals. With very few natural predators, the Japanese hydra was a symbol of an abundant and thriving natural ecosystem to the people of Japan.

Today, human industrial encroachment, the construction of dams, power plants and bridges, along with industry on the Chikugo River on the island of Kyushu has destroyed most of the Japanese hydra's natural habitat, although the Japanese government has created a dragon sanctuary for the Yamato no Orochi in Fukuoka Prefecture. Today, specimens of the hydra can be found in zoos in Tokyo and Okinawa where the Dragon Species Plan (DSP) is attempting to re-introduce these dragons into the wild.

SPECIFICATIONS
Hydridae chikugous

Size: 10' (3m)

Distribution: Southern Japan, South Korea

Recognition: Bright red and black markings

Habitat: Rivers and streams

Diet: Small reptiles, fish

Common names: Yamato no Orochi

Conservation status: Critically endangered

CEREBRUS HYDRA

The cerebrus hydra almost entirely exists as a bred species in dragon rookeries. Many draconologists today argue that the cerebrus was never a natural species, but rather a hybrid of a hydra and a drake. The cerebrus, however, has been documented since ancient Greece and whether it was wild or selectively bred may never be known.

Unlike other hydra species, the cerebrus is able to growl and bark like a hound. It is also unique in that it is born with three heads and is unable to grow new ones.

Today, this rare and ferocious dragon is kept as a pet by only a select few wealthy collectors and breeders, but it can be found in zoos and nature parks around the world. The World Dragon Protection Fund works tirelessly every year to find and disrupt the cruel practice of cerebrus pit fighting that the dragon is most famously bred for.

SPECIFICATIONS
Hydridae cerebrus

Size: 6' (2m)

Distribution: Northern Mediterranean, Greece, Albania and Turkey

Recognition: Short stocky body, three heads

Habitat: Hills and grasslands

Diet: Small mammals and rodents

Common name: Houndguard

Conservation status: Extinct in the wild

Medusan Hydra

The medusan hydra lives in swamps and tidal basins where it burrows into the mud, concealing its large body. The heads enable it to catch eel, crawfish and small animals as they pass by. In some legends, the medusan hydra was often mistaken for a nest of snakes. They have been hunted to near extinction, mostly due to misunderstanding and fear.

SPECIFICATIONS
Hydridae medusus

Size: 10' (3m)

Distribution: Mediterranean Basin, Africa, India

Recognition: Array of small snake heads in worm-like body

Habitat: Swamps and tidal basins

Diet: Eel, crawfish, small animals

Common name: Serpent's Nest

Conservation status: Critically endangered

Winged Hydra

The winged hydra was a three-headed flying hydra native to the regions of eastern Europe. It is believed to have gone extinct somewhere around the 16th century.

SPECIFICATIONS
Hydridae wyvernus

Size: 30' (9m)

Wingspan: 40' (12m)

Distribution: Caucasus Mountains of Eastern Europe and Asia

Recognition: Wings and three reddish heads

Habitat: Rocky, mountainous regions

Diet: Unknown

Common name: Zmey Gorynych

Conservation status: Extinct

INDIAN HYDRA

The Indian hydra is a large hydra species that spends its life wading in the slow-moving, murky waters of the rivers in South Asia. The Indian naga is regarded as a sign of fertility and prosperity throughout much of the Indian subcontinent and Southeast Asia. This is probably because a healthy river with plentiful food attracts hydra.

SPECIFICATIONS
Hydridae gangus

Size: 30' (9m)

Distribution: South Asia, India, Myanmar and Thailand

Recognition: Red, crested heads

Habitat: Rivers and lakes

Diet: Fish, small mammals, reptiles

Common name: Naga

Conservation status: Endangered

MARINE HYDRA

LERNAEN HYDRA

The Lernaen hydra lives in the boughs of trees, allowing its heads to drape down to catch its food. It can remain still for hours, waiting to spring. The use of the entire nest of its heads may be required to subdue larger prey.

Hydra Skeleton
A unique, highly porous bone structure allows for the advanced regeneration of the hydra.

SPECIFICATIONS
Hydridae lernaeus

Size: 20' (6m)

Distribution: Mediterranean islands

Recognition: Multiple serpent heads, serpent body

Habitat: Treetops

Diet: Small rodents, fish, birds

Common name: Tangle Worm

Conservation status: Critically endangered

Although almost all the species of hydra live near bodies of water where they hunt for fish, and are able to swim to a varying degree, the marine hydra is the only hydra species that lives its entire life in saltwater and can swim great distances, only exiting the water to lay its eggs. Having evolved webbed feet and an oversized liver to create buoyancy, the marine hydra cruises the tropical shallow reefs of the South Pacific hunting tropical fish and shellfish. Often coming into competition with other predators such as sharks, the hydra is well armored and protected by its multiple heads to ward off attacks.

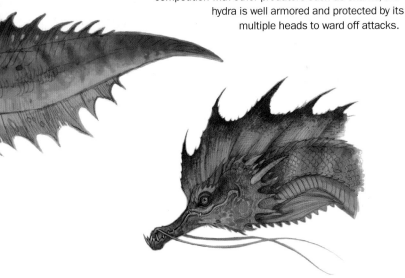

SPECIFICATIONS
Hydridae oceanus

Size: 20' (6m)

Distribution: Archipelagoes of Melanesia

Recognition: Multiheaded marine hydra

Habitat: Shallow saltwater reefs

Diet: Fish

Common names: Ocean Hydra, Phillip's Hydra

Conservation status: Endangered

Sonoran Basilisk
Pencil and digital
14" × 22" (36cm × 56cm)

BASILISK

Draco lapisoclidae

BIOLOGY

The eight-limbed, poisonous basilisks of the world's deserts are one of the most extraordinary of the dragon groups.

The basilisk is a member of the Terradracia order, or flightless dragons. This multilimbed reptilian beast of about 10' (3m) is famous for its ability to petrify anyone who gazes into its eyes. This magical power has been much dramatized in literature and mythology over the centuries, but actually, it is not the animal's gaze that petrifies, nor is there any magic involved. The basilisk is able to shoot a jet of neurotoxin from a gland in the corner of its eyes (not unlike the horned toad of North America). This toxin has the ability to paralyze the basilisk's prey, rendering it defenseless.

The dragon species of basilisk is not to be confused with the South American species of lizards within the family Basilicus. These small reptiles are related to the iguana in the order of Reptilia.

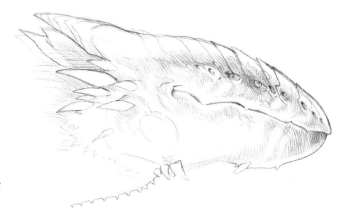

Basilisk Eyes
Although it is often depicted as having many eyes like a spider, the basilisk possesses only one set of eyes. It does have as many as eight sets of false eyes. These orifices are used to sense vibrations in the earth and locate its prey.

Basilisk Habitat
Basilisks can be found in caves and outcroppings in desert regions from Southern California and Texas to Central America, as well as deserts around the world.

Basilisk Feet

The basilisk has four sets of powerful, broad feet that allow it to quickly burrow in the sandy soil. It's been documented that it can excavate up to 3 cubic feet (85L) of soil a minute, creating elaborate lairs and tunnels under the desert.

Sensory organs much like that of a crocodile allow for heightened sensitivity of the skin, allowing the basilisk to sense prey and movement in the dark.

BEHAVIOR

Because of its multiple limbs, the basilisk is a lumbering and slow-moving animal. The legs allow for adept burrowing of its underground lairs, where it is able to wait to ambush its prey. These underground burrows also allow the basilisk to withstand the harsh temperatures of its environment. Despite the legends of its famous gaze, the basilisk has terrible eyesight and is practically blind. The basilisk detects its prey with its sensitive nasal orifices.

The bite of the basilisk is also dangerous, containing the same neurotoxins from the eye glands. This highly poisonous and dangerous animal is brightly colored in broad stripes, indicating itself to larger predators as poisonous. The heavy armor further protects the basilisk from enemies.

The basilisk is a solitary creature. The female basilisk can lay up to six eggs at a time with an average life span of twenty years.

HISTORY

Since the basilisk is a creature from the remote deserts of Arabia and Africa, classical and medieval European reports of the creature are sporadic and unreliable. Bestiaries of this time relate the basilisk to the cockatrice (see chapter 1); this mistake is even made in accounts as recently as the early 20th century.

The basilisk's habitat was once a remote and inhospitable land. Now, with the intrusion of humans upon the desert landscape, attacks from basilisks have become more common. Along the border between the United States and Mexico in Big Bend National Park, Texas, there are nearly 100 reported fatalities a year from basilisk attacks. Park rangers assert that the number is probably much higher since attacks in the backcountry usually go unreported.

Basilisk Egg, 8" (20cm)

The basilisk egg can withstand harsh environments.

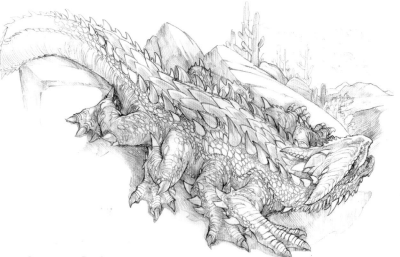

Dangerous Predator

Lying in wait for its prey, the basilisk can sense movement in the soil up to 328' (100m). Extreme caution must be taken while hiking in the desert.

SONORAN BASILISK

The Sonoran basilisk of the southern United States and Mexico is the largest and most common species of basilisk. It is rarely seen in the open, and despite its large size, it easily remains hidden among the rocks and in the sand during daylight hours.

SPECIFICATIONS
Lapisoclidae incustambulus

Size: 12' (4m)

Distribution: Southwest United States, Mexico

Recognition: Tubular body, spiked back

Habitat: Desert

Diet: Carnivore

Common name: Stone-Eye Dragon

Conservation status: Threatened

STRZELECKI BASILISK

Native to the outback of Australia, the Strzelecki basilisk was first documented by the British transcontinental Burke and Wills expedition of 1860. It is classified with the Latin name of the Yandruwhanda tribe of native Australians who lived in the region of the Strzelecki and Simpson Deserts in the Lake Eyre basin of South Australia. Hunted to near extinction by British colonists in the 19th century, the Strzelecki basilisk has returned to sustainable numbers after its listing on the endangered species list in the late 20th century.

SPECIFICATIONS
Lapisoclidae yandruwhandus

Size: 10' (3m)

Distribution: Australia

Recognition: Heavy tail, small forearms

Habitat: Desert

Diet: Carnivore

Common names: Burke's Basilisk, Australian Basilisk

Conservation status: Endangered

Saharan Basilisk

This large, long thin basilisk is a quick hunter, hiding in the shifting sands of the Saharan desert dunes, whipping out to attack its prey. Although longer than its Sonoran cousin, the slight Saharan weighs less. It often lies just below the sand, waiting to sense the vibrations of passing creatures. The Saharan's light frame allows it to travel long distances above the sand without sinking into it.

SPECIFICATIONS
Lapisoclidae solitudincursorus

Size: 20' (6m)

Distribution: North Africa

Recognition: Long, thin body; eight legs; cranial crest

Habitat: Deep desert

Diet: Lizards, small mammals

Common name: Desert Runner

Conservation status: Endangered

Gobi Basilisk

The Gobi basilisk, or cave basilisk, is the smallest member of the Lapisoclidae family. Native to the rocky terrain of China's Gobi desert, this basilisk makes its lair in rocky ledges and caves where it will sit in hiding for weeks at a time, hunting insects, small lizards and even bats with its long striking tongue. Like other species of basilisk, the Gobi basilisk has very poor eyesight, hunting by using its false eyes to detect movements in air pressure and temperature to locate its prey. The use of poisonous neurotoxins in its saliva help incapacitate its prey and ward off predators.

SPECIFICATIONS
Lapisoclidae sagittavenandii

Size: 6' (2m)

Distribution: Central China

Recognition: Eight legs; long prehensile tail; thick armored plates

Habitat: Rocky caves and ravines in the Gobi desert

Diet: Insects, small reptiles and birds

Common names: Arrow-Hunter, Cave Basilisk

Conservation status: Endangered

THAR BASILISK

The Thar basilisk is a docile, slow-moving, omnivore basilisk that poses little danger to humans and their livestock, burrowing into the sandy soil of the deserts of the Arabian Peninsula to India foraging for roots and tubers that make its principle diet.

The Thar basilisk once ranged from the Arabian desert in modern-day Saudi Arabia to the Thar Desert in India. The opening of trade along the Silk Road during the crusades gave rise to the many medieval legends of basilisks found in European bestiaries. It has been a favorite subject of hunts throughout the Roman, Turkish, Persian and British Empires, domination of the region. Accounts of using basilisks in gladiatorial contests go back to the reign of Emperor Tiberius. As a result, the Thar basilisk was classified as extinct in 1903 until an expedition by the American Institute of Natural Sciences discovered a living specimen in 1947 in Western India.

Today, the Thar basilisk has been returned to survivable populations in some of its former habitats, protected by several sanctuaries and conservation groups, with successful breeding in captivity in zoos around the world contributing to the conservation success with the Dragon Survival Plan (DSP).

SPECIFICATIONS
Lapisoclidae armisfodiensus

Size: 8' (2.5m)

Distribution: Middle East, Pakistan, India

Recognition: High-arched back; large, layered scales from back to tail; short tail

Habitat: Desert

Diet: Tubers, roots, fungi, insects

Common names: Arabian Basilisk, Raja Dragon, Armored-Digger, Sultan's Basilisk

Conservation status: Critically endangered

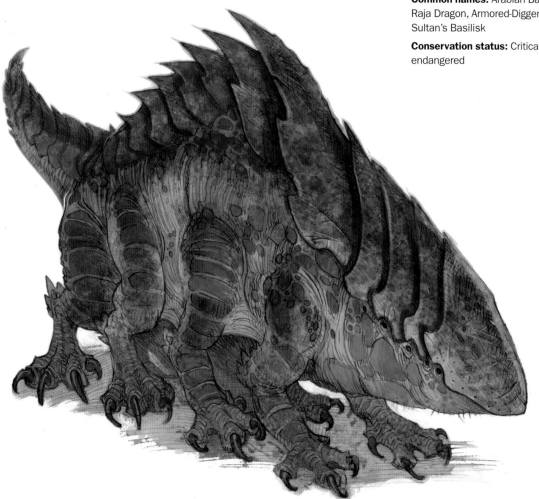

AETNA SALAMANDER

The Aetna salamander has been associated with the island of Sicily and its majestic volcano for centuries. Favoring the fresh ash and loose rock of recent eruptions for its nesting areas, the Aetna salamander is often encountered when trying to reclaim an area from ash fall. Construction efforts can sometimes be held up while Aetna salamanders are relocated to more rural areas.

SPECIFICATIONS
Volcanicertade erumperus

Size: 20"–30" (51cm–76cm)

Distribution: Sicily and the Tunisian Coast

Recognition: Strong, pincerline jaws

Habitat: Loose soils in and around active thermal areas

Diet: Insects, small mammals, olives

Common name: Catania Crawler

Conservation status: Endangered

Vesuvius Salamander

The Vesuvius salamander is adapted to life in the water as well as on mountainsides. They are used to traveling among the warm volcanic vents along Italy's west coast, and they have become predators in the warm summer waters of the Tyrrhenian Sea. Its tall dorsal fin propels it, whiplike, through the currents. During winters, the Vesuvius will migrate to heated geothermal areas to mate.

Specifications
Volcanicertade Tyrrhennius

Size: 18"–22" (46cm–56cm)

Distribution: West coast of Central Italy

Recognition: Tall dorsal fin; single nasal horn

Habitat: Rocky coastline

Diet: Shore birds, shellfish

Common name: Sail Fin Dragon

Conservation status: Uncommon

Fuji Salamander

Not to be confused with the Fuji dragon in the family Draco cathaidae, this salamander is related only by general origin area. The Fuji salamander avoids light and seeks the deep heat of geothermal venting. It burrows deep into crevices along volcanoes and near thermal steam vents. In Japan, during the Kamakura and Muromachi periods (1185–1568), it was highly sought for the reputed medicinal properties of its flesh and bones.

SPECIFICATIONS
Volcanicertade aestu ignis

Size: 12"–14" (30cm–36cm)

Distribution: Japan, Philippine Sea

Recognition: Heavy, paddle-like tail; large crest cap

Habitat: Coastal volcano regions

Diet: Insects

Common name: Suruga Salamander

Conservation status: Uncommon

Kilauea Salamander

The kilauea salamander basilisk is contained within the subgenus *Volanicertidus*. It's a small basilisk usually not exceeding 12" (30cm) in length, and it commonly lives in environments of extreme heat, such as the volcanoes of Hawaii. A salamander basilisk can withstand temperatures up to 800°F (427°C). It is believed that these temperatures allow the creature to live where predators are unable to enter, leaving the salamander basilisk in relative safety.

SPECIFICATIONS
Volcanicertade incendiabulus

Size: 8"–12" (20cm–31cm)

Distribution: Hawaii

Recognition: Sharp, beak-like jaw; lawyered scales from head to tail

Habitat: Volcanoes, campfires, stoves

Diet: Carrion

Common names: Touch Worm, Cook' Craw Worm

Conservation status: Least concern

Cloud Dragon
Pencil and digital
14" × 22" (36cm × 56cm)

ARCTIC DRAGON
Draco nimibiaqidae

BIOLOGY

The *Nimibiaquidae* family of dragons includes all of the flightless, furred dragon species. They are serpentine creatures that ply the frozen wastes north of the Arctic circle, hunting seals, small whales and even polar bears. Although greatly resembling the Asian dragon species (see chapter 2), Arctic dragons differ significantly in their biology in that they all grow fur, and do not have the wing frills particular to the Asian dragon. Covered in a sheath of thick fat and a coat of fur, the Arctic dragon blends into its environment to ambush its prey. Despite its fur covering, all Arctic dragon species have a hide of intricate scales. Ranging across the globe, the Arctic dragon species are found in northern Canada and the tundra of Siberia, while some species migrate as far south as China and the northern United States.

Arctic Dragon Head

Arctic Dragon Habitat
The frozen wastes of northern China, Russia and North America are the Arctic dragon's natural home.

Arctic Dragon Egg, 8" (20cm)
In the fall, Arctic dragons venture south to lay their eggs and wait out the winter in milder regions. Once hatched in the spring, the dragonlings travel with their mother to northern hunting grounds.

Arctic dragons have played prominently in pop culture. Falkor the Luck Dragon in *The Neverending Story*, as well as Appa in the animated series *Avatar*, could be Arctic dragons. Despite these roles as pets or companions, the Arctic dragon is one of the most dangerous animals in the world.

BEHAVIOR

Survival in the northern climates of the Arctic is harsh. Most species of the Arctic dragon are omnivorous to take advantage of any food available. The larger species of Arctic dragons will hibernate in the winter, burrowing deep into the polar snows to make its lair. Snow serpents are cunning hunters, artfully using the concealment of arctic fog and cloud-shrouded peaks to camouflage itself. With reduced eyesight, snow serpents hunt by smell and the feel of long whiskers. This allows the animals to hunt effectively even in blizzard conditions. This ability to float silently through the clouds has led to many of the beautiful images of Arctic dragons depicted in Asian art.

HISTORY

The fur of the Arctic dragon is prized for its beauty, softness and ability to insulate. Northern cultures throughout the world have elevated the Arctic dragon to supernatural status. In China, the storm dragon is believed to bring prosperity and good luck because its presence frightens off other large predators, such as wolves and wyverns.

Arctic Dragon Foot
The Arctic dragon's feet are large and partially webbed, similar to a polar bear's. Its long, curved claws are ideal for grasping prey.

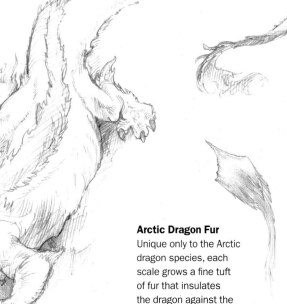

Arctic Dragon Fur
Unique only to the Arctic dragon species, each scale grows a fine tuft of fur that insulates the dragon against the harshest environments.

Zmey Dragon

The Arctic white dragon was once so prolific that it ranged as far west as Moscow, giving the dragon its name Zmey (Russian for dragon). Today the zmey dragon's distribution is limited to the northern territories of Western China, Tibet and Bhutan. The white dragon graces the flag of Bhutan, where it is a symbol of national identity. It was once a dominant dragon in high northern elevations, but its gradually diminishing numbers have now reduced sightings to rare occurrences. Its hide is sought after as a black market product. Steps have been taken to protect its remaining population, but enforcement against poaching is nearly impossible over such geographically difficult and far-ranging territory.

Specifications
Nimibiaqidae bhutanus

Size: 20' (6m)

Distribution: Western China, Russia, Tibet, Nepal, Bhutan

Recognition: White coloration and markings; prominent cranial horn

Habitat: Alpine mountains

Diet: Kilin, mammals

Common names: Bailong, White Dragon, Unicorn Dragon, Autumn Dragon, Western Dragon

Conservation status: Critically endangered

Kilin Dragon

The kilin species of Arctic dragons more greatly resemble big horn sheep in size and habitat, and they are particular only to Asia.

Staying high in the Alpine mountains for safety, kilin are adept climbers, leaping agilely from promontories in pursuit of food or to evade larger predators. Kilin are one of the few dragon species that live in herds, often gathering in tight groups on high mountains for warmth.

Although kilin are shy and elusive animals, many Asian communities see them as good luck. They are also famous for being companions to wizards in Asia. Mountain-dwelling sorcerers, monks or hermits come into contact with kilin and domesticate them in rare instances. Today the kilin herds are reduced in Northern China and Russia, but in the fall they can still be seen leaping in the mountain passes.

Specifications
Nimibiaqidae dracocaperus

Size: 5' (1.5m)

Distribution: Northern Asia and Russia

Recognition: Long mane from nose to tail; long-haired boots

Habitat: Mountainous Arctic terrain

Diet: Omnivore

Common names: Kirin, Kylin, Quilin, Quirin, Chinese Unicorn

Conservation Status: Endangered

GREAT WHITE KILIN

In 1968 the rare and elusive great white kilin was first documented by Russian naturalists in remote Northern China in the Qilian Mountains, making it the most recent dragon to be discovered.

Today the great white kilin is considered one of the most endangered dragon species. The World Dragon Protection Fund and the International Organization for the Conservation of Dragons has inaccurately placed it on the extinct list more than once. It is believed that up to twelve great white kilins are left alive in the wild today. The Chinese government has gone to great lengths to protect the dragon from poachers, since multimillion-dollar bounties have been offered for their horns, which are prized as a magical compound that can cure any disease. No attempt has been made to breed the great white kilin in captivity.

SPECIFICATIONS

*Nimibiaqidae
dracocaperus-dujiaoshous*

Size: 8' (2.5m)

Distribution: Northern Asia, Russia

Recognition: White markings; branching antlers

Habitat: Mountainous subalpine terrain

Diet: Omnivore

Common names: Spirit of the Forest, Great White Stag, Ruru

Conservation status: Critically endangered

COOKS DRAGON

The cooks dragon is one of the more prolific of the Arctic dragons to have survived human development and hostile climates in Eastern Russia and Alaska. The cooks dragon was first discovered in 1778 on Captain Cook's third expedition to the Pacific Northwest and Alaska.

The cooks dragon's main source of food is the elk and polar bears in its region. It makes its lairs in ice caves in the mountains. Socially a solitary dragon, the cooks dragon does live with its mate during the nesting, incubation and hatchling period, using its limited fire-breathing ability to keep its eggs warm. The families will break up to look for new mates and lairs after the hatchlings are old enough to leave the nest. As for many of the larger dragon species, the average lifespan of the cooks dragon is around 100 years.

SPECIFICATIONS
Nimibiaqidae kamchatkus

Size: 8' (2m)

Distribution: North Atlantic Rim, Kamchatka, Alaska

Recognition: Black coloration and markings

Habitat: Arctic mountains

Diet: Elk, polar bears

Common names: Xaunglong, Black Dragon, Winter Dragon, Dragon of the North, Chukchi Dragon

Conservation status: Endangered

Cloud Dragon

This large, flightless dragon is one of the true masters of the north. With one of the largest populations located among the glaciers of Greenland, the cloud dragon has assumed a near mythological place in draconian lore. It is rarely seen, but evidence of its power and presence are constantly brought home by sailors and explorers who have ventured into its northern habitat. There have been recent reports of a small colony newly establishing itself on the shores of Labrador.

Specifications
Nimibiaqidae ryukyuii

Size: 20' (6m)

Distribution: Eastern China, Japan

Recognition: Green, curly mane

Habitat: Coastal regions, tropics

Diet: Tropical fish, sealife

Common names: Quilong, Green Dragon, Spring Dragon, Eastern Dragon

Conservation status: Critically endangered

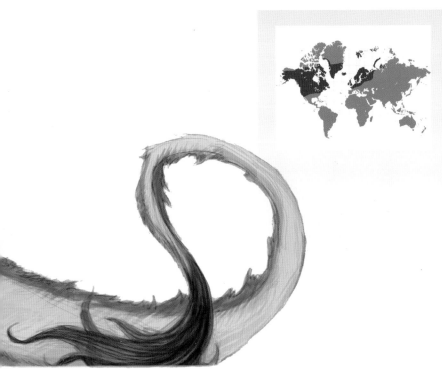

SPECIFICATIONS
Nimibiaqidae nebulus

Size: 35' (11m)

Distribution: North America, Northern Europe, Greenland

Recognition: Serpentine tail; gray fur

Habitat: Arctic tundra

Diet: Seals, cetaceans

Common name: Icelord

Conservation Status: Critically endangered

HOKU DRAGON

Once flourishing throughout the tropical islands of the Eastern China Sea and the archipelago of Japan, today the hoku dragon survives in strictly protected sanctuaries on a few isolated habitats in the Ryukyu Islands. As human population growth, industry and warfare devastated the hoku's environment, the dragon's food supply dwindled. As a result, the numbers of these dragons drastically diminished in the 20th century. The hoku dragon was one of the first animals to be registered on the endangered species list in 1973.

STORM DRAGON

The rare storm dragon is the largest member of the Nimibiaqidae family. Common is Asian art, the storm dragon is a symbol of prosperity, good fortune and the Chinese emperor. Its appearance has been associated with the imperial family for centuries, and it has been featured in many of the culture's colorful legends. A close relative to the cloud dragon, the storm dragon has a larger, more serpentine form. Diminishing habitat has led to fewer reported sightings in recent years.

LUCK DRAGON

The luck dragon is one of two Arctic dragon species that does not live in the Arctic region, but rather in southern China. Because of human development in the 20th century, the luck dragon became extinct in its historical range from Shanghai to Hong Kong. Today the luck dragon only survives in the wild in a protected mountainous forest reserve on the southern Chinese tropical island of Hainan.

The luck dragon is extremely reclusive and is difficult to spy in the wild. Eco-tourism to Hainan to see the luck dragon is extremely popular. Many people leave prayers and wishes for the luck dragon to grant. Historically, Buddhist monks believed the enigmatic luck dragons to be protectors of the forest.

SPECIFICATIONS
Nimibiaqidae xishus

Size: 15' (5m)

Distribution: Southern China

Recognition: Red markings

Habitat: Mountainous jungles

Diet: Birds, reptiles, small mammals

Common names: Chilong, Summer Dragon, Red Dragon, Southern Dragon

Conservation status: Critically endangered

SPECIFICATIONS

Nimibiaqidae tempestus

Size: 50' (15m)

Distribution: Northern Asia

Recognition: Gray mane; tail longer than body

Habitat: Arctic tundra

Diet: Carnivore

Common name: Emperor Dragon

Conservation status: Critically endangered

American Banyan Wyrm
Pencil and digital
14" × 22" (36cm × 56cm)

WYRM

Draco ouroboridae

BIOLOGY

One of the most infamous families in the dragon class, the wyrm has been perhaps the most feared creature throughout all human cultures. The wyrm is distinguished by both its lack of wings and legs, although the lindwyrm species do have small vestigial legs. Looking much like an armored snake, wyrms can reach tremendous sizes of more than 50' (15m), although the average wyrm only reaches 25' (8m) due to harsh hunting practices that have cut down their populations. Natural enemies of alligators, crocodiles and hydra, wyrms live along swampy river banks and salt-water tidal basins, hunting large animals such

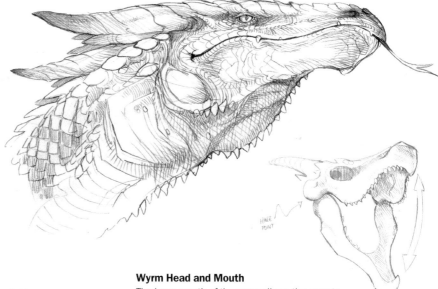

Wyrm Head and Mouth
The large mouth of the wyrm allows the maw to be opened wide enough to swallow its prey whole.
The long snout contains a large nasal cavity, which, along with the sensitive tongue, gives the wyrm an excellent sense of smell.

Wyrm Habitat
Wyrms tend to live in temperate to tropical climates, especially in lowlands and wetlands where they lie in wait for their prey.

as boar and deer. Although not able to breathe fire, the wyrm is able to spray a cloud of misted poison that can paralyze and blind its prey, allowing the animal to swallow its quarry whole.

BEHAVIOR

The wyrm is a solitary and viciously territorial animal. Burrowing its lairs under the roots of large trees alongside rivers and lakes, it lies in wait for prey to come to the water to feed. The wyrm sprays a plume of noxious gas that paralyzes or dazes its prey, giving the wyrm enough time to capture and coil around the animal. Using the powerful muscles of its body, the wyrm constricts around its prey, suffocating and crushing the animal to death. The wyrm then typically swallows its prey whole. The eastern species of wyrm typically hide in tree branches and dangle down, waiting for prey to pass by. Large specimens of wyrm have been discovered with the remains of cattle in their stomachs. One report actually claims that an Indian drakon (*Ouroboridus Marikeshus*) was discovered at more than 100' (30m) and containing the remains of an elephant.

Movement of the Wyrm
The coiling, serpentine motion of the wyrm can be seen in these sketches, where the body is similar to a whip.

Wyrm Egg, 10" (25cm)
A clutch of 4 to 6 wyrm eggs laid in the roots of a tree will be intensely guarded by the mother.

HISTORY

Almost every culture in the world has a long mythological history of giant serpents. The famous accounts of Python, who is slain by Apollo in classical mythology, Nidhogg of ancient Norse mythology and the serpent in the Garden of Eden are all assumed to have been wyrms. All of these creatures are large serpents that live on or around trees. Such creatures would have been a terrible threat to early human cultures whose survival relied upon settlements along rivers. Other fables that are accredited to wyrms are the Questing Beast of King Arthur and the dragon that swallowed Saint Margaret. The wyrm possesses spiritual symbolism in many ancient religions in the form of the serpent eating its own tail, or Ouroboros, symbolizing infinity or the circle of life, from which is derived the wyrm's family name.

Today, the European lindwyrm is on the endangered species list, while the American banyan wyrm is openly hunted in the southern United States. The African striped wyrm and the Indian drakon are believed to cause hundreds of deaths a year to tribal river peoples, and is hunted and trapped. The hide of the wyrm is used for shoes and other leather goods. Many ancient cultures use the wyrm's poison as a sacred drink, allowing them to have visions.

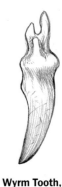

Wyrm Tooth, 3" (8cm)
The wyrm has small teeth in relationship to its body. The teeth are not used for hunting or killing, rather for grasping prey and swallowing.

EUROPEAN KING WYRM

Closely related to the American banyan wyrm and a cousin of the European lindwyrm, the European king wyrm (or great wyrm) went extinct sometime in the 15th century. Skeletal remains exist of some specimens believed to have reached over 100' (30m). This dragon is most likely the basis of the Lambton Wyrm legend.

SPECIFICATIONS
Ouroboridae rex

Size: 100' (30m)

Distribution: Europe

Recognition: Blue ridges; red eye area; long whiskers; short, spiral horns

Diet: Carnivore

Common names: Great Wyrm, Azure Serpent

Conservation status: Extinct

AMERICAN BANYAN WYRM

Reaching lengths of 50' (15m) in maturity, the American banyan wyrm is one of the few natural competitors of the American alligator. Long known and revered by Native American cultures, this dragon quickly developed mythic status among early Spanish explorers in what is now the lower United States and Central America, who grew to fear its size and speed. These days, it continues to provide new legendary tales from its habitat in the vast swamplands of the American South.

SPECIFICATIONS
Ouroboridae americanus

Size: 50' (15m)

Distribution: Southeast United States, Central America

Recognition: Green and blue markings; cranial horns

Habitat: Marsh, wetlands, rivers

Diet: Carnivore

Common name: Bayou Serpent

Conservation status: Low risk

Wyrm Skeleton
The skeletal framework of the wyrm resembles a stretched-out spring or coil.

African Striped Wyrm

The African striped wyrm, like its drakon cousin, is a large, territorial wyrm that lives along the riverbanks of Africa. It was first catalogued by the British explorer Linvingstone in 1873 after researching the local legends and myths of a giant dragon that lived in the nearby river. The African striped wyrm can reach sizes rivaling the Indian drakon and is nearly as dangerous, but because of the sparsely populated regions of its habitat it is not responsible for nearly the number of human deaths as its Indian cousin.

Hunted by native tribes that live in the African river basins, the African wyrm is prized for its hide, teeth and poisonous secretion. Its meat is also a staple of many indigenous people.

Specifications
Ouroboridae kafieii

Size: 100' (30m)

Distribution: Central and Southern Africa, Madagascar

Recognition: Orange and black stripes

Habitat: Rainforest, jungle, wetlands, rivers

Diet: Carnivore

Common name: Tiger Wyrm

Conservation status: Low risk

ASIAN MARSH WYRM

Like its wyrm cousins, the Asian marsh wyrm makes its home along the riverbanks and marshes of Asia. The bristling spines along its body and two vestigial legs anchor the wyrm into its burrow where it will bury itself into the muddy river banks, waiting for its prey to venture too close and fall into its crushing jaws to be swallowed whole.

Unique to the Asian wyrm is its ability to navigate large bodies of saltwater, allowing the species to travel throughout the archipelagoes of Southeast Asia and survive extreme weather such as tsunami and monsoons that may devastate its habitat.

The Asian marsh wyrm became known as the hell wyrm to American soldiers during World War II and the Vietnam War, with both the Japanese and the North Vietnamese using them in traps to harass advancing American soldiers in the wetlands and rice paddies of Asia.

SPECIFICATIONS
Ouroboridae nahanguisus

Size: 50' (15m)

Distribution: Southeast Asia, Oceana

Recognition: Green coloring; spiny surface; two small "arms"

Habitat: Marshland, river deltas, swamps

Diet: Carnivore

Common names: Hell Wyrm, Pit Wyrm, Mekong Viper, Naha Wyrm

Conservation status: Low risk

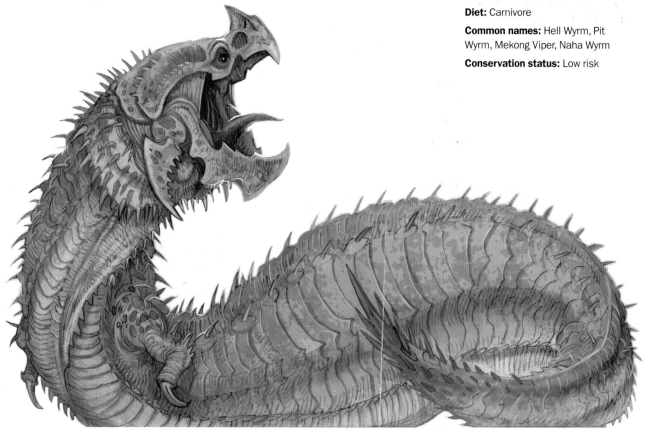

EUROPEAN LINDWYRM

The European lindwyrm has been the subject of legends and myths for centuries in the countries where it was once living. It is believed that this wyrm species ranged from Italy to Ireland living in a colder habitat than its wyrm cousins, causing this species not to grow nearly as large. The two legs of the lindwyrm allow the dragon to burrow into lairs to hibernate through the European winters. Changes in climate in Europe during the medieval period, combined with extensive overhunting, drove the lindwyrm into extinction around 1800.

INDIAN DRAKON

The Indian drakon is one of the fiercest and largest terrestrial dragon species ever recorded. Reaching lengths of over 150' (45m), the huge serpentine dragon lies in wait along the river banks and marshes of India, Pakistan and Sri Lanka, striking at its prey with immense speed, rendering it immobile with noxious gas breath and then swallowing it whole. On the Indian subcontinent, the drakon is responsible for more human deaths than any other animal, making the drakon the most dangerous dragon species to humans in the world.

The transportation or breeding of drakons is strictly forbidden. Illegal poaching and selling of juvenile drakons to pet owners in Europe and America is widespread. Specimens discovered in the wild in the United States have been known to grow to dangerous sizes and have been competing in the ecosystem with the American banyan wyrm.

Size: 20' (6m)

Distribution: Europe

Recognition: Long serpentine body; long snout; two vestigial legs

Habitat: Rivers, wetlands

Diet: Birds, lizards, fish

Common names: Fafnir, Whiteworm

Conservation status: Extinct

SPECIFICATIONS
Ouroboridae marikeshus

Size: 100' (30m)

Distribution: South Asia

Recognition: Heavily armored snake body

Habitat: Wetlands, rivers

Diet: Cattle

Common name: Ajagari

Conservation status: Low risk

South American Coatyl
Pencil and digital
14" × 22" (36cm × 56cm)

COATYL

Draco quetzalcoatylidae

BIOLOGY

The coatyl is of the order of feathered dragon (Pennadraci-formes). Long believed to be a purely mythological creature, the coatyl is revered as a holy animal to the native people of its habitats. The coatyl family is one of the smallest in the Draconia class, consisting of only a few of the feathered, limbless dragons.

The Egyptian coatyl or serpent also lives in and around the ancient ruins of Giza and has four brightly colored gold and turquoise wings. The phoenix, which makes its habitat in the monuments and temples of Persia and Mesopotamia, is bright crimson with breathtaking ruby feathers. The eggs of the phoenix are unique in that they have a very thick shell to protect the chicks from the desert heat and predators.

Male Coatyl Behavior
The crown plumes and wattle of the coatyl are only on males, which they use to attract the attention of females.

Coatyl Habitat
The South American coatyl makes it habitat in the deep South American jungles. This seclusion has allowed for the relative safety of the species.

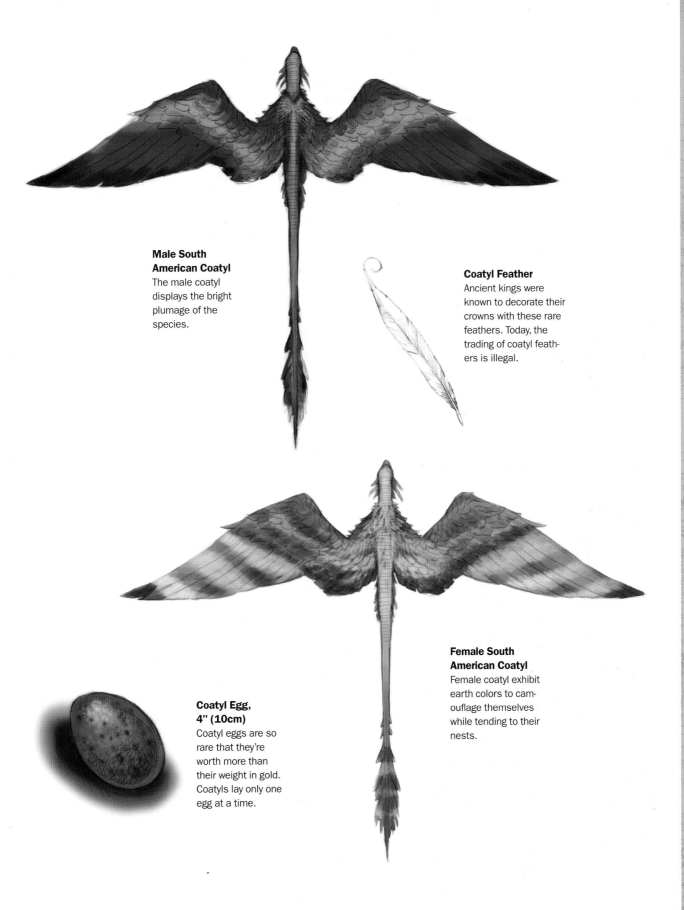

Male South American Coatyl
The male coatyl displays the bright plumage of the species.

Coatyl Feather
Ancient kings were known to decorate their crowns with these rare feathers. Today, the trading of coatyl feathers is illegal.

Female South American Coatyl
Female coatyl exhibit earth colors to camouflage themselves while tending to their nests.

Coatyl Egg, 4" (10cm)
Coatyl eggs are so rare that they're worth more than their weight in gold. Coatyls lay only one egg at a time.

This shell is also impenetrable to the baby phoenix. The heat of fire, however, cracks the shell open, releasing the newborn phoenix, as if it was born out of the flames. The parent phoenix may refuse to leave the nest, becoming consumed in the fire. Because of this dangerous birthing technique, the phoenix is extremely rare, and some believe extinct.

Behavior

Since it makes its nests in the rocky overhangs and crevices of ancient Aztec and Inca ruins from Belize to Peru, the coatyl is said to have a magical relationship with the peoples of Central and South America. Now biologists understand that the various coatyl species actually live in a symbiotic relationship with humans. Humans feed and protect the coatyl, revering it as a spiritual animal while the species, in turn, keep out vermin.

Only the male coatyl possesses the colorful feathered wings that have become so prized by poachers over the centuries and led to their decline in numbers. The coatyl lays only one egg at a time, and the average life span is fifty years.

History

For millennia, the coatyl was considered to be a mythological creature. It was first discovered by Spanish conquistador Diego Velázquez de Cuéllar in 1513; the last South American coatyl in captivity died in 1979 at the Lima Zoo. The coatyl is believed by many Aztecan religions to be the earthly embodiment of the god Quetzalcoatyl, which is the root of the family's Latin name. The coatyl also refers to the massive pterosaur, quetzalcoatlus, discovered in Texas in 1971.

Once populating the kingdoms of the Aztec and Inca people in vast numbers, the introduction of European animals and diseases in the 16th century decimated the species, along with the magnificent culture they inhabited. Today the International Coatyl Fund works to return this ancient creature to its former glory.

SOUTH AMERICAN COATYL

The South American coatyl has a large serpentine body that's surmounted by colorful wings. It makes its habitat in the ancient ruins and jungles of the South American continent, where it was discovered by western explorers in the late 19th century. Although revered as a holy creature by South American natives, it was hunted to the brink of extinction for its brightly colored plumage.

Today, the South American coatyl is a protected species, but in the wide expanse of the jungles discovery and apprehension of poachers has proven extremely difficult.

SPECIFICATIONS
Quetzalcoatylidae aztecus

Size: 6' (2m)

Wingspan: 8' (2.5m)

Distribution: South America

Recognition: Brightly colored plumage and head crest; serpentine body

Habitat: Mountainous jungle rainforests

Diet: Small mammals, lizards, insects, birds

Common names: Fly Dart, Sky Prism

Conservation status: Critically endangered

EGYPTIAN SERPENT

Making its nests in the oases along the northern Nile River, the Egyptian coatyl has lived in close contact with humans since ancient times. Having four wings of gold and turquoise markings, the beautiful dragon was often depicted in the hieroglyphics and jewelry in the tombs of Egyptian pharaohs, giving rise to the dragon's Latin name. In 1922, a 3,000-year-old mummified Egyptian serpent was discovered in the tomb of Tutankhamun.

Today the only known specimens of Egyptian serpent are found in the Cairo Zoo. Despite repeated attempts, the mated pair (named Anthony and Cleopatra) have been unable to produce any eggs, leading some specialists to believe they will be the last Egyptian serpents in the world.

SPECIFICATIONS
Quetzalcoatylidae ramessesii

Size: 6' (2m)

Wingspan: 6' (2m)

Distribution: Northwest Africa

Recognition: Four brightly colored wings with turquoise and gold markings; head crest

Habitat: Desert regions, river oases

Diet: Small mammals, insects, lizards

Common names: Pharaoh's Dragon, Rameses' Dragon

Conservation status: Extinct in the wild

PHOENIX

First encountered thousands of years ago in Persia (modern day Iraq), the phoenix, like its *Quetzalcoatylidae* cousins, has a symbiotic relationship with the humans in its habitat. According to ancient texts, the phoenix was one of the exotic animals kept in the menagerie in the Hanging Gardens of Babylon built by King Nebuchadnezzar in 7th century B.C.

Strict protections are now enforced in dragon sanctuaries in Iraq, and the International Coatyl Fund works to reintroduce hatchlings from captivity back into the wild. However, contemporary conflicts continue to threaten this beautiful dragon to near extinction.

SPECIFICATIONS
Quetzalcoatylidae nebuchadnezzarus

Wingspan: 8' (2.5m)

Distribution: Mesopotamia

Recognition: Serpentine body; bright red plumage

Habitat: Palm groves, river oases

Diet: Small mammals, reptiles, insects

Common names: Babylonian Dragon, Gilgemesh's Dragon

Conservation status: Critically endangered

British Spitfire Dragonette
Pencil and digital
14" × 22" (36cm × 56cm)

DRAGONETTE

Draco volucrisidae

BIOLOGY

Few images evoke more romance and excitement than the dragon rider on his steed. For centuries the dragonette has been bred by civilizations all over the world for a variety of purposes, from the diminutive courier dragonette to the powerful war dragonettes.

The dragonette is a bipedal dragon with powerful back legs and small front legs used for digging and nest building. It also possesses expansive batwings for graceful and agile flying. The dragonette usually stands about 6' (2m) at the shoulder and is 12' (4m) in length with a 20' (6m) wingspan. A vegetarian herd species from the open plains, and much less intelligent than its larger dragon cousins, the dragonette was domesticated by early civilizations and today is common throughout most of the world. Bred into hundreds of breeds, the dragonette can be found in a variety of patterns and sizes to fit its many functions.

Dragonette Head
Dragonettes have large eyes that allow for peripheral vision while grazing. The short muzzle and small teeth are designed for biting and chewing grass.

Dragonette Habitat
From the plains and grasslands of Australia to the mesas of the western United States, dragonettes gravitate in groups to rock cliffs for safety and breeding.

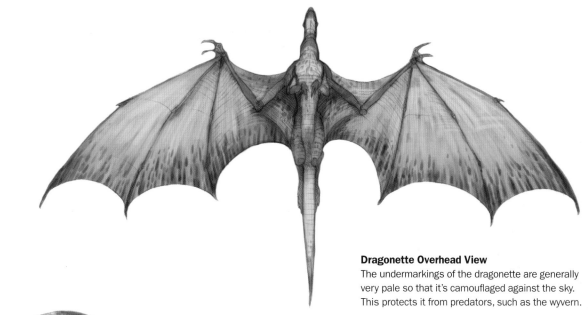

Dragonette Overhead View
The undermarkings of the dragonette are generally very pale so that it's camouflaged against the sky. This protects it from predators, such as the wyvern.

**Dragonette Eggs, 10"
(25cm); 1½" (38mm)**
A dragonette's egg size can vary widely depending on the size of the species.

BEHAVIOR

Dragonettes are unique within the Draconia class in that they live within flocks (or flights) that can grow into thousands of animals. Very social and docile creatures, they commonly build their nests on the high plateau mesas of the Central United States, Eastern Europe and Australia. A whole flight of dragonettes may migrate thousands of miles between seasons to follow the food supply and reach its breeding grounds.

HISTORY

Varieties and breeds of the dragonette can be found in almost all regions of the world. Although not as intelligent or easy to train as horses, dragonettes are considered a working breed and have long been used for transportation and military use. Napoleon's Dragoniers were amongst the most famous, as well as the British Royal Dragon Guard, the German Drachwaffe and the American Dragon Express Mail Service. Most dragonettes have been used by military commanders to survey the battlefield and carry messages. After World War I, the dragonette was replaced by the airplane and today the dragonette is solely kept by breeders and racers.

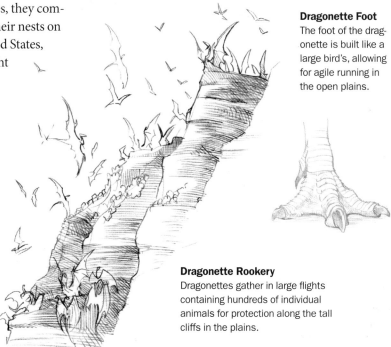

Dragonette Foot
The foot of the dragonette is built like a large bird's, allowing for agile running in the open plains.

Dragonette Rookery
Dragonettes gather in large flights containing hundreds of individual animals for protection along the tall cliffs in the plains.

AMERICAN APPALOOSA DRAGONETTE

Famous in the American frontier in the 19th century, these hardy dragons were used by American cavalry and the Dragon Express Mail Service to explore the western United States. Their manageable size and ability to be trained made them very sought after for tasks ranging from herding to long-distance mail delivery. Their increased usage led to the formation of the 103rd Light Dragon Cavalry Division, with service out of Fort Missoula, Montana, during the late 19th century.

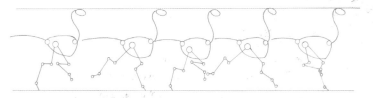

Dragonette Locomotion
This sequence of wire-frame drawings illustrates how the dragonette runs on its powerful hind legs. Notice how its center of gravity is deep over its knees.

SPECIFICATIONS
Volucrisidae chyennus

Size: 12' (4m)

Distribution: Northeastern America

Recognition: Soft brown coloration; small head; fin on bottom of tail

Habitat: Forested river areas

Diet: Herbivore

Common names: Pinto Dragon, Delaware Drifter

Conservation status: Uncommon

COURIER DRAGONETTE

This diminutive dragonette was used for centuries to transport information across great distances at high speed. Most famous during battles, when it was necessary to send orders to units on the edges of troop movements, they were used with great effect during the American Revolution, when Colonial troops used native dragonettes to maintain communications across their spy network.

SPECIFICATIONS
Volucrisidae zephyrri

Size: 3' (1m)

Distribution: Worldwide

Recognition: Small size; bright red color

Habitat: Forests, though adapted to more extreme conditions

Diet: Herbivore

Common names: Ruffle, Dartwing

Conservation status: Uncommon

MESSENGER DRAGONETTE

Similar to the courier dragonette, this species has been used among a variety of breeds to carry small parcels and important documents across distances. The messenger was used extensively in Japanese feudal society, and its migration, along with other aspects of Asian culture, to the west coast of America brought it into common use during California's Gold Rush days. The messenger is attracted to unusual objects and collects materials for nesting from the flotsam and jetsam that washes in with the tides.

SPECIFICATIONS
Volucrisidae vector

Size: 5' (1.5m)

Distribution: Pacific coast

Recognition: Small size; upright posture; batlike ears

Habitat: Shorelines, sandy beaches

Diet: Herbivore

Common name: Beachcomber

Conservation status: Common

ABYSSINIAN DRAGONETTE

This beautiful, thoroughbred Arabian breed of dragonette is famous for its speed and agility. Domesticated by desert nomads, the Abyssinian has long been seen as a status symbol among the upper echelon of Middle Eastern society. It is particularly difficult to capture, making it both rare and highly prized in captivity.

SPECIFICATIONS
Volucrisidae equo

Size: 12' (4m)

Distribution: Middle East, Southern Asia

Recognition: White mottled coloring

Habitat: Arid highland regions

Diet: Herbivore

Common names: Desert Racer, Wind of Iram

Conservation status: Critically endangered

WAYNESFORD DRAGONETTE

The workhorse of the dragonette family, the waynesford is also known as the shiredragon. These dragons have been used throughout centuries as pack animals and work dragons to transport goods over long distances. Over time, the waynesford dragonette become so highly sought after as a draft animal that its native population is no longer found in the wild. While the species continues to be popular, all current descendants are from ancestry that have been bred and raised in captivity.

SPECIFICATIONS
Volucrisidae gravis

Size: 15' (5m)

Distribution: Northern hemisphere

Recognition: Strong, stout build; short neck and tail; warm color tones

Habitat: Forested areas

Diet: Herbivore

Common name: Shiredragon

Conservation status: Bred in captivity only

North American Wyvern
Pencil and digital
14" × 22" (36cm × 56cm)

WYVERN
Draco wyvernae

BIOLOGY

By far one of the most dangerous and ferocious members of the dragon class, the wyvern is sometimes referred to as the dragon wolf.

Averaging 30' (9m) long with a 30' (9m) wingspan, the wyvern has two legs and a spiny tail surmounted by a poisonous stinger. Its durable hide of armored scales gives the wyverns ample protection to fight off other predators and even larger dragons when fighting in a pack. Although the wyvern does not possess a breath weapon, his poisonous stinger, powerful body and ferocious maw of razor-sharp teeth make it a formidable foe.

BEHAVIOR

The wyvern is a social animal that lives in packs of up to twelve individuals, ranging over a territory many hundreds of miles in area. Hunting in packs allows for more successful attacks on prey, which include animals

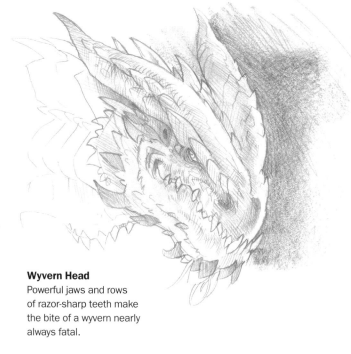

Wyvern Head
Powerful jaws and rows of razor-sharp teeth make the bite of a wyvern nearly always fatal.

Wyvern Habitat
The wyvern habitat ranges all over the world's alpine regions. Although extinct in the Alps, the Asian wyvern is moving westward.

Wyvern Egg, 12" (30cm)
The average female lays six eggs, though less than half of wyvern hatchlings will survive to adulthood.

such as moose, elk, bear, caribou and (its favorite) the dragonette. Pack society also enables the wyvern to fight off other packs of wyverns competing for hunting territory.

During the rutting season in the fall, the wyvern male wing patterning becomes vibrant in order to attract a female. The competition between males is fierce, often resulting in the death of rivals. The wyvern, like other temperate-climate dragon species, hibernates through the winter when food is scarce.

HISTORY

The wyvern is the beast responsible for most of the injuries throughout history reported as dragon attacks. It is believed by contemporary accounts and period artwork that the beast slain by Saint George was, in fact, a wyvern and not a dragon.

The European wyvern went extinct in the 1870s. The last known specimen was placed on tour with P. T. Barnum's circus until 1898 and is now in permanent exhibit at the Field Museum of Natural History in Chicago. The Asian and other wyvern species are still flourishing and many casualties are reported each year as new developments encroach upon their habitat.

Expert Hunter
Hunting over large expanses of wilderness, the wyvern is a danger to people and their livestock.

Wyvern Tracks
Wyvern tracks are abundant in mountainous hunting territories. If you see them while hiking, leave the area immediately!

Sea Wyvern

The sea wyvern is the only species of wyvern that lives next to bodies of water. Often living in small rookeries or packs of up a dozen specimens, it congregates near rocky terrain located close to bodies of water where it can fish using its stingered tail to capture its prey. Although the sea wyvern's tail produces poison like its cousins, the lethality of the poison is much less than other species because it is primarily used for fishing.

Asian Wyvern

Often confused with many species of Asian dragons, the Asian wyvern is as dangerous as its wyvernidae cousins. It uses its whip-like stingered tail to injure its prey, thus giving it the Latin name "swordtail." The Asian wyvern is known to mark its territory by using its tail to lash bark from the trees on the edge of its range. These marked trees are called "sword-struck" and serve as warnings to challengers of all species.

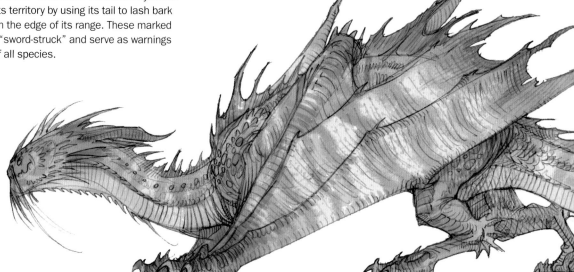

SPECIFICATIONS
Wyvernae pocnhmachus

Size: 20' (6m)

Distribution: Western Asia, India

Recognition: Elongated snout; blue markings; stingered tail

Habitat: Rivers, lakes, seashores

Diet: Piscivore

Common names: King Fisher, Tail Fisher

Conservation status: Endangered

SPECIFICATIONS
Wyvernae jianwaibaii

Size: 20' (6m)

Distribution: Central and southern Asia

Recognition: Long serpentine body with frills

Habitat: Mountain jungles

Diet: Carnivore

Common names: Swordtail, Chainwhip

Conservation status: Rare

GOLDEN WYVERN

The golden wyvern is one of the more prolific of the wyvern species making its habitat in the reclusive mountains of eastern Asia and Russia.

Its massive clubbed tail is used primarily as a rutting weapon to ward off potential mates. The tails tend to be much larger on the males and can be used as offensive weapons to incapacitate prey with poisoned barbs.

Its short muzzle and sharp teeth are used to rend the meat off of the bones of its prey.

SPECIFICATIONS
Wyvernae zolotokhvostus

Size: 25' (8m)

Distribution: Eastern Asia, Russia

Recognition: Golden/brown markings; spiked clubbed tail

Habitat: Mountains

Diet: Carnivore

Common name: Golden Tail

Conservation status: Near threatened

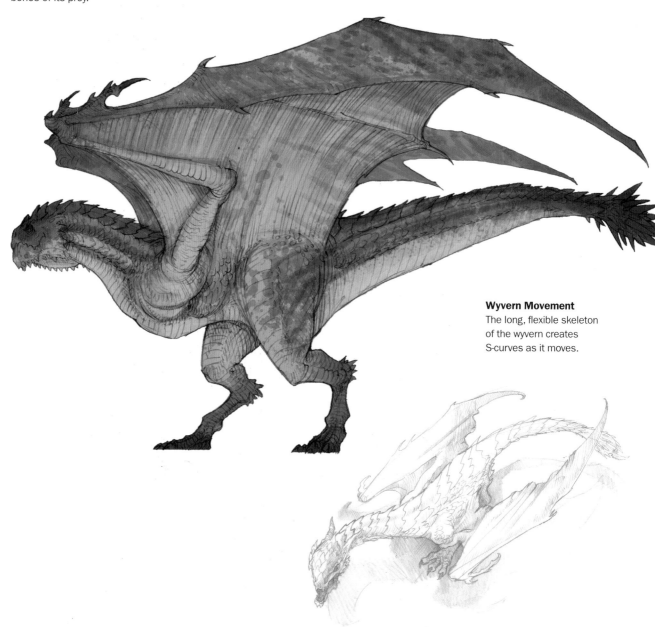

Wyvern Movement
The long, flexible skeleton of the wyvern creates S-curves as it moves.

NORTH AMERICAN WYVERN

When first encountered by western explorers to the interior of North America, this wyvern proved itself a force to be reckoned with. Native to the Rocky Mountains, it regularly made the passage increasingly difficult for settlers and those working the western plains. It was not until the turn of the 20th century, with the disappearance of their main prey—the American Bison—that the wyverns' numbers also fell to levels that allowed for safer, more frequent human travel.

SPECIFICATIONS
Wyvernae morcaudus

Size: 30' (9m)

Distribution: North American mountains

Recognition: Ringed markings along back edges of wings; barbed, thorny tail

Habitat: Mountainous and alpine regions

Diet: Carnivore

Common names: Dragon Wolf, Death Tail

Conservation status: Endangered

Wyvern Tail
The wyvern's tail is covered with spines that can be projected at an enemy, as well as a poisonous stinger capable of killing an ox.

Dedication

This volume is dedicated to the readers who have found the world of *Dracopedia* to carry them further in their own creativity.

To the O'Connor family, and to Samantha and Madeline; may you soar with the dragons.

CONTRIBUTORS

We thank the following individuals for their contributions to this project:

Golden Dragon Head, page 15
Dan dos Santos
Design and color

Spirit Dragon, page 26
Samantha O'Connor
Color (design by William O'Connor)

Fuji Dragon, page 27
Pat Lewis
Color (design by William O'Connor)

Hammerhead Sea Orc, page 34
Richard Thomas
Color (design by William O'Connor)

Frilled Sea Orc, page 35
David O. Miller
Color (design by William O'Connor)

Flying Sea Orc, page 36
Donato Giancola
Design and color

Striped Sea Orc, page 37
Donato Giancola
Design and color

Manta Sea Orc, page 37
Jeff A. Menges
Design and color

Ishtar Drake, page 89
Jeremy McHugh
Color (design by William O'Connor)

African Striped Wyrm, page 130
Mark Poole
Design and color

Abyssinian Dragonette, page 148
Christine Myshka
Color (design by William O'Connor)

Waynesford Dragonette, page 149
Scott Fischer
Color (design by William O'Connor)

a content + ecommerce company

Other fine IMPACT books are available from your favorite bookstore, art supply store or online supplier. Visit our website at fwmedia.com.

23 22 21 20 19   5 4 3 2 1

Distributed in the U.K. and Europe
by F&W Media International LTD
Pynes Hill Court, Pynes Hill, Rydon Lane,
Exeter, EX2 5AZ, United Kingdom
Tel: (+44) 1392 797680
E-mail: enquiries@fwmedia.com

ISBN 13: 978-1-4403-5384-0

Edited by Noel Rivera and Amy Jones
Designed by Clare Finney
Production managed by Debbie Thomas

Metric Conversion Chart

To convert	to	multiply by
Inches	Centimeters	2.54
Centimeters	Inches	0.4
Feet	Centimeters	30.5
Centimeters	Feet	0.03
Yards	Meters	0.9
Meters	Yards	1.1

ABOUT THE AUTHOR

William O'Connor is author and artist of the best-selling *Dracopedia* book series, as well as illustrator of more than five thousand illustrations for the gaming and publishing business. His 25-year career allowed him to work with such companies as Wizards of the Coast, IMPACT Books, Blizzard Entertainment, Sterling Publishing, Lucasfilms, Activision and many more. In addition, he won more than thirty industry awards for artistic excellence including ten contributions to *Spectrum: The Best in Contemporary Fantasy Art* and ten Chesley nominations. William taught and lectured around the country about his unique and varied artwork and was a regular contributor to the popular art blog Muddy Colors. He exhibited his work at numerous industry shows, such as Illuxcon, New York Comic Con and Gen Con.

For more information about William O'Connor, his books and art, visit wocstudios.com

To see more art and videos about *Dracopedia*, visit these online sites:

Dracopedia at Facebook: facebook.com/dracopedia
The Dracopedia Project: dracopediaproject.blogspot.com
Dracopedia YouTube Videos: youtube.com/user/
    wocstudios1

IDEAS. INSTRUCTION. INSPIRATION.

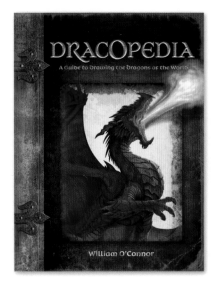
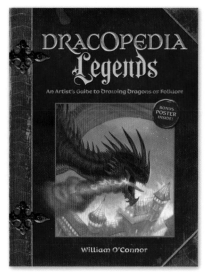
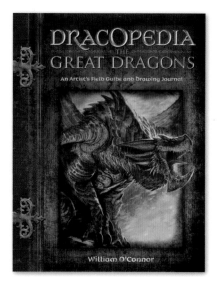

Check out these IMPACT titles at IMPACTuniverse.com!

These and other fine IMPACT products are available at your local art & craft retailer, bookstore or online supplier. Visit our website at impactuniverse.com.

Follow IMPACT for the latest news, free wallpapers, free demos and chances to win FREE BOOKS!

Follow us!

IMPACTUNIVERSE.COM

- Connect with your favorite artists
- Get the latest in comic, fantasy and sci-fi art instruction, tips and techniques
- Be the first to get special deals on the products you need to improve your art

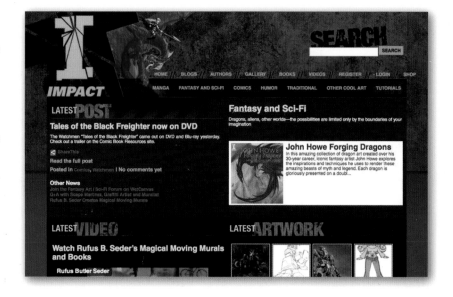